Omega for the Pack

The Stars of the Pack – Book I
N.J. LYSK

Palm Hearts
PalmHeartsBooks@gmail.com
ISBN: 978-1-916630-23-9

The Stars of the Pack series (Chronologically)

Companion series:
Runt of the Litter
Paper Kisses

Also available in German, French, Italian, Dutch, Spanish, Portuguese and bilingual learner editions.

Omega for the Pack

Chapter 1

R ay stepped forward and bowed. He didn't raise his gaze from the floor and he kept still. His heart was racing, but at least he could appear calm. Not that he could hide his scent, of course. Every alpha in the meeting hall knew he was scared, and he could smell them in turn: eager and hungry. For him. Because he was an omega and he was ready to mate.

"Raymond," his uncle said, almost gently. Only then did Ray look up. Only for a second, not long enough to decipher his expression. He couldn't have taken the pity, not then. He focused his gaze on the side of the stubbled cheek of the First Alpha of his pack. The man who controlled his life now. He had to show respect, show he was paying attention when an alpha spoke to him. "It's true. You've come into your own."

It was just about the politest way of putting what was happening to Ray's body: The changes had just started that would turn him from a beta—all children were betas—into an omega. From a boy into... No, he'd never be a man now, omega males weren't men. In the old days, werewolves just used the animal term for them: bitches. But of course nobody would say that in public now. Now they were omegas, or breeding males—mates for the alphas who took them or the pack that formed around them. Whatever you called people like Ray, one thing was true: They were rare. Most werewolves were born of females of the species.

At eighteen, Ray had heard of less than half a dozen adult male omegas. One of them had had a mate, but the rest... well, Ray knew what alphas said: It was such a waste to let a fully grown man go to waste by breeding for a single alpha. That wasn't what male breeders were meant for, they argued; they were born strong and big so a new pack could form around them. Ray shivered, aware of the heavy gazes on him, aware that he was all of 6′2″ and broader at the shoulders than men older than him. It had always been an advantage to him before, keeping other wolves—notoriously rowdy—from challenging him, but size wasn't an advantage to an omega male.

"I have decided to grant the request for a new pack," his uncle announced. Ray's stomach dropped. He was fully dressed—jeans and two shirts and his parka on top—but he suddenly felt chilled to the bone, and he had to lock his knees to keep himself upright. He had been hoping, he realised. Stupidly, he'd thought... But of course it didn't matter that his uncle was first alpha of their pack; he couldn't give a healthy male omega to a single mate—no matter how much he might have wanted to protect him.

In a pack as large as theirs, a split had become inevitable. Many would argue Ray's new status was a direct result of the need for an omega to form a new pack. Once upon a time, when he'd been sure he'd come out of childhood an alpha, Ray had thought of forming a new pack himself. He'd never thought of what an omega might feel at the prospect. As far as he'd been told, omegas in heat needed an alpha to breed with or they would go out of their mind with lust.

But he wasn't in heat, not yet, and arousal was the furthest thing from his mind as he felt the crowd around him stir impatiently, like predators about to jump their prey. His uncle didn't speak the names of the alphas he'd chosen. They must have already known. Ray kept his gaze focused on the wall behind his uncle's left shoulder. It wasn't because he thought he'd be reprimanded if he looked away; he was just too terrified of finding who they were. The men who would get him.

Omegas' mates were traditionally chosen by their parents, not the first alpha. An omega's parents didn't have to listen, of course, but most parents would still *ask*. But Ray's dad had passed away when he was little, and his uncle had looked after Ray and his mum and his siblings since then. It was only right that he would choose for Ray now, his mum—herself an omega—had said. She was sure he would make a better choice than she could. Maybe she'd known there was no way Ray would get a single mate. Maybe she hadn't wanted to be the one to choose this for him.

There was a hand on his elbow, barely cupping the delicate bone there. Ray startled like he'd been hit. The owner of the hand reached out and caught his parka, bunching it up and bringing him close again. Ray froze, the scent of alpha filling his nostrils—and even though he knew what was going to happen, it just loosened something in him. An omega wolf knew it was safe with an alpha because an alpha would do anything to keep them. And then Ray's shell-shocked brain finally processed the rest of the scent and his head snapped up. He couldn't help it.

Because this wasn't a stranger: It was Ray's best friend.

There was a noise like a whimper as their eyes met: Josh's hazel brown as always, but without a hint of his usual good humour. There was just warmth there. Concern. Ray's face felt like it was going to combust, and the sheer humiliating knowledge of what he must smell like to Josh now was like a weight he could barely stand. Josh wasn't touching his skin, and he already felt too hot, burning with both terror and... Lowering his head felt like tearing something, his eyes stinging as he pulled his gaze away from his friend's. No, not his friend. Not anymore. Because Josh being allowed to touch him here and now could only mean one thing: He was going to be Ray's alpha.

"Hey," Josh said softly, like they were alone. Except he'd never spoken to Ray in that tone before. He'd always teased and dared, never... Ray's fear was rapidly leaving him and now all he could feel was anger. He'd thought Josh was his friend, but why would a friend ask for *this*? "Don't freak out," Josh went on, so strangely careful—like he didn't know Ray anymore, like he thought now that Ray was an omega, he couldn't handle things. "I've got your back."

And with that, Ray yanked himself violently away, taking a step back and baring his teeth. Josh's eyes widened in surprise and alarm, but he wasn't angry. Before, he'd have responded to such overt hostility with the same, but of course an alpha wouldn't attack an omega. He wasn't worth fighting anymore, just fighting *over*. He glanced around and found the faces of the other alphas who'd stepped forward. They weren't as close as Josh, but they were surrounding him and the wolf got confused for a second.

Until very recently, the only reason alphas would have surrounded him like this was to attack him. In a flash, Ray was transforming. His clothes were left in a heap as he turned tail and ran.

He didn't know if any of the alphas in the room tried to stop him, but they didn't succeed.

Of course it was Josh who found him, naked and huddling in a cave where they'd played as children. Ray had felt his presence, but the cave didn't have another exit and there was nowhere else for him to go, anyway. Packs weren't just blood, but loyalty and protection, and a lone wolf didn't live long.

He heard a rustling sound but only understood it when Josh announced, "I've left your clothes."

Then he heard his friend step away. So he was allowed to get dressed before he had to come and face the music. He hesitated a moment longer: When he put on those clothes, he'd have no excuse to stay in the cave anymore. The chase would be over, and he'd be caught.

But then he realised that every second he took, he was proving them right, proving an omega was afraid. He didn't like the cards he'd drawn, but that didn't mean he couldn't face it. He couldn't choose. He couldn't walk away. *Fine*. But he wasn't going to quiver and cringe like a limpet. It didn't matter what they did to him, they couldn't change who he was.

And Raymond Halley might not be an alpha, but he wasn't a coward.

When he emerged, Josh turned clumsily in his direction. Ray saw him swallow thickly. They hadn't seen each other at all since before Ray had presented. Ray didn't know what he had expected, but Josh looked the same: tanned skin over thick muscle, luminous hazel eyes, his lips curved on the cusp of a smile even though there was nothing happy about his expression. But he was looking at Ray in a completely new way—half like he was afraid of him, half like he was afraid of startling him again. Josh, who'd delighted in scaring the crap out of him after every horror movie and in every haunted house. Ray wondered if he could punch an alpha, as long as it wasn't his alpha yet. *Yet...* He had to exhale and look away for a moment to collect his thoughts.

Josh was only a little taller than Ray, so little the only way to tell was if they stood back to back, not that he'd ever stopped ribbing Ray about it before. Now he'd think...

"Ray," his friend said. He was flushed enough to be visible, even in the twilight. "Your uncle told me, and I wanted to help," Josh explained. "I promise. I just want to help."

Ray snorted, bitter and hurt, and turned away for a moment to gather the strength to speak. It was harder now. His wolf knew it was in front of an alpha, it *wanted* to submit. "I'm sure that's *all* you want."

"It's all I want," Josh insisted, and it rang true, heart steady, breathing agitated but even. "And if I want something else later, it will only be to help you."

Ray almost laughed. It would not have been a happy sound, and he was so full of anger and indignation that he didn't dare let any of it out for fear of what else might escape. "So you're doing me a favour," he finally said. This time he didn't even try to look at Josh. He couldn't fight his wolf and himself at the same time.

"I'm doing what I have to do to keep you safe," Josh replied.

"Safe?" he repeated. "Did you hear what my uncle said?"

"You know you will be safe. No alpha would ever harm you."

"Then why? Why you? Why—"

"Because I *know* you, Ray, and I know what you want. And I can keep it all from overwhelming you. What you have to do... it doesn't have to be your whole life."

And that was when the wolf lost the battle: Ray threw himself at Josh. He got him in the gut, hard enough to leave him whizzing, and almost hit him again before he realised that Josh wasn't fighting back.

"Hit me," he demanded, shaking Josh hard enough to make his teeth rattle. It wasn't the first fistfight they'd got into with each other, and it wouldn't be the last. They would never really hurt each other, of course. That was part of the appeal, they could let loose with someone strong enough to take it.

"I can't!" Josh panted, trying to push him away, but not hard enough to succeed.

"What the fuck do you mean *you can't*?" Ray spit out, pushing him in turn, hard enough to tumble him to the ground.

Josh looked up at him, not attempting to get to his feet. "That fucking hurt, Raymond, but I couldn't... I can't."

"You said you wanted to help," Ray reminded him. Slowly enough not to startle, Josh got to his knees, then his feet until he was looking Ray in the eye again.

"I need... I've just lost everything. I can't..."

Josh took a decisive step forward and pulled until Ray was stumbling into his arms. It was only the familiar roughness of the gesture that kept Ray from pushing him away.

"No, you fucking haven't," Josh said indignantly. "You have me."

Ray shook in his arms, with fury, or loss, or desperation. "But the others..."

"They're good guys, Ray. Your uncle consulted with me. They're all guys you know; guys we can trust."

Ray thumped his head against Josh's collarbone. "How can there be good guys for this?"

He felt so lost, untethered from reality as he knew it, with only Josh to keep him grounded. Except this wasn't Ray's best friend, the guy who had his back and knew all his embarrassing teenage stories. This guy, smelling unmistakably of alpha, was going to fuck Ray. Not just that, he'd watch as the rest of the new pack did as well. And if the stories were true, Ray would be happily spreading his legs for it. He shuddered, and Josh's arms tightened around him.

"We need to get back," he told Ray. He didn't apologize for it, but he didn't try to move away. It was such a typical Josh thing to do: remind Ray of his duty, but leave it up to Ray to decide to go through with it.

Of course they had to go back; they were waiting for him. Had all the alphas been waiting all this time? Ray didn't think he could face them again.

"We don't need to go back to the meeting hall, just... We can get the others, then we can go to the site. It's on the other side of the river," Josh explained. Like Ray could possibly give a fuck about where he was going to be fucked and mated. He pushed out of Josh's embrace as roughly as he'd been pulled into it. But the intent wasn't the same. He could see by Josh's stricken expression that he knew it too.

"Let's go," he decided. There was little enough he would be able to decide from then on.

There were four men lingering outside the meeting hall. That wasn't odd, there was usually someone hanging about there. The odd thing was that nobody else was about, and the meeting couldn't have ended that long ago. They were being given privacy, Ray guessed. It made him want to scream. They wouldn't give him a choice, or even tell him in advance, but the alphas got to see him alone? Nobody had even considered how that would feel for Ray: to have to face these men, all at once, knowing he belonged to them.

Josh stopped right behind him. Despite everything, Ray was glad he was there.

"Do you remember me?" one of the alphas asked.

He was leaning against the building, casually displaying the strength of his biceps. His dark eyes and hair made his skin look pale under the lamplights illuminating the baroque front of the town hall, but Ray knew it was a shade darker than his own, as if the product of a constant tan that nobody could have maintained in Northern England.

Ray did know him. His family had stopped by a few years back and ended up staying. It was one of the many reasons the pack was now too large to be managed. They'd played football together. He was a great forward, fast and versatile; but Ray and Josh's team had kicked their arse last time they'd faced them anyway. He couldn't remember his name, he realised, and almost wanted to laugh at the absurdity of it all.

"Iesu," his former rival offered, taking a step forward and extending his hand. Ray clasped it in his automatically. And then the name clicked in his mind.

"Iesuvel." He'd thought it was a pretty name, and Ray had a good memory for pretty things. He couldn't remember his last name, which really say a lot about how messed up the whole situation was.

This earned him a smile. Ray wanted to smile back. It could have been normal, except of course the guy was pleased Ray remembered him because...

Ray turned away, to the right. Suddenly all he wanted was to get this done. He could bear anything as long as he could be alone afterwards, just get a minute to process. And then he raised his eyes and the surprise almost made him stumble.

"Gabriel," Ray gasped.

How had he missed him? Gabriel was even taller than Ray, blond and blue-eyed, and strong enough that it showed even standing in a badly lit street at night. He was Ray's cousin once removed, and for reasons nobody quite understood he'd never sought a mate despite being at least a decade past presentation. He'd always been kind to Ray when he'd been a kid: taking the time to shoot some ball with the kids at parties, and distracting adults from broken china until they could disappear.

"Nobody told you about this," his cousin said then, between gritted teeth. "You smelled so shocked, Ray. If I'd known..." His eyes slid past Ray, glaring at Josh behind him. Ray had never seen Gabriel angry before, nor even heard of it. Gabriel's response to other people's irritation tended to be to roll his eyes and suggest a solution.

But he was way beyond angry now. Of course he was: an alpha's first instinct towards an omega was to protect. This affected Josh, too, and his usually affable friend snapped at the accusation. "When was I supposed to tell him? He's been holed up at home since... he presented."

Ray was about to try to say something to calm them down—he wasn't sure what—when someone else saved him the trouble.

"But the First Alpha is your uncle, isn't he? He said you were basically his own son. Why wouldn't he have told you?"

The speaker was slighter than Ray himself, not a small man by any means—werewolves rarely were—but compactly built and shorter. He stepped back as soon as Ray looked at him, looking startled. He had wolf golden eyes, barely enough brown in them to keep humans from staring and his hair was a dark copper, glinting red in the harsh artificial light. Ray had never seen him before in his life.

"And why the fuck would I lie about it?" Ray snapped. He had no patience to lose and to have a stranger question intimate family matters was beyond unbearable at this point.

"Sorry," the man said softly, raising his hands defensively. "I never said you were lying, just thinking aloud." Ray scowled at him a moment longer, hoping it'd help him remember where they'd met. He would have believed he was a wolf of his uncle's pack—he could smell that much even through the overwhelming alpha pheromones—but that was all there was to it.

"You said I knew them," he told Josh, not bothering to lower his voice or turn to look at him.

"Alec is actually on the 'you can trust' list," Josh explained, sounding apologetic.

"And why would I trust him?" Ray asked, eyes fixed on the golden-eyed stranger. He'd put his hands down and decided to keep his mouth shut. He didn't seem the macho alpha type who'd want to order an omega around like a servant, but that didn't mean Ray had any reason to accept him.

"I vouched for him," Gabriel offered. Ray was about to ask for more information when the fifth man stepped out of the shadows and spoke.

"And so did I."

Only Josh's hold on his arm kept Ray from either rushing forward or trying to get away. "What the fuck? Is this some sick joke?"

He was going to murder Josh for this. In front of him was none other than the only boy in the pack who'd never cared how big Ray was—he would always show up looking for a fight. He was so blindly furious that he couldn't even speak.

Not before Sergi did. "This is going to sound pretty stupid," Sergi told him in a tone devoid of all the usual aggression, "but I've had a crush on you for... I don't know, years."

"What?" Ray said, so stunned he actually swayed. His anger hadn't dissipated completely but he was mostly too confused to hold onto it.

Sergi's skin was too dark to show his blush in this light, but he looked unhappy and uncomfortable—as one might be when asking one's rival to bend over. He was so far from the cocky and defiant bully Ray knew; it was hard to believe they were the same person.

"I know I was a jerk, but I was a kid, and you were... I was freaked out about liking a guy," he gritted out finally, eyes skittering away.

Of course it was fine for a male alpha to want a male omega, but the rest of the time... Well, the survival of the pack didn't allow for indulging one's 'inclinations'. Ray had known this all his life and kept his attraction to men quiet while he spent his teenage years exploring the soft curves of girls. Of course, males in general were expected to be straight, but not omegas. Omegas weren't supposed to care who mounted them when they were in heat; that was why relatives or the pack arranged matings for them at their own convenience.

"So you treated me like shit," Ray concluded.

Sergi raised his eyes to him, glaring for all he was worth. "You were shitty right back."

And it wasn't like Ray could deny that, but he hadn't signed up to screw Sergi, had he? "And now you thought you'd kill two birds with one stone? Get to fuck me and fuck me over?"

His old rival recoiled, looking as shocked as if Ray had accused him of murder. "No! I want... Look, it's not like nobody else is interested. Your friend said I could ask, but if you don't want me..."

Being offered a choice now was nothing short of cruel; if it existed, why hadn't anybody asked him before? If he asked his uncle, he'd probably tell him that he had figured Ray wouldn't care. An unmated omega would need only one thing: an alpha.

"Funny how nobody thought to ask me that before," Ray spat anyway. He didn't deserve this and he didn't have to pretend otherwise. At least for now, the wolf wasn't making him show submissiveness to the alphas.

Sergi might have changed tactics, but he hadn't lost any of his stubbornness. "Well, I'm asking you now."

"We need to take this somewhere private," Gabriel interrupted, and Ray flinched.

His cousin sighed. "To talk," he clarified, looking too sympathetic for Ray's taste. Sure, he had good reason to freak out, but that didn't mean he wanted Gabriel's pity.

Ray nodded. Gabriel's flat was only a few streets away, in the town proper outside of official pack territory—Gabriel's inexplicable little rebellion. But even closer to the human area, the streets were pretty empty this late at night. Lanchester was a sleepy English town where nothing ever happened—if you didn't count half the population turning into wolves every full moon and running wild in the fields and forests around town. Maybe that's what kept the locals inside this late, some sort of leftover instinct from when humans had known about shifters—before science had told them the truth was impossible.

Ray had always felt safe in these streets. He'd always known he could get back home where nothing bad could happen to him with his pack to back him up.

He hadn't counted on needing protection *from* his pack.

He shoved his hands in his pockets, and kept his gaze front, trying not to listen to the sounds the five alphas made, or worse, smell their scents. Except for Gabriel in the lead and Josh a step behind him, they were all following quietly, but their presence was impossible to ignore. Maybe it was mating instincts, maybe it was dread.

Gabriel was twenty-nine and—despite being single—had moved out of his parents' house long ago. Ray vaguely remembered his uncle's displeasure at his son's humanish behaviour. What had made Gabriel change his mind after all these years?

Gabriel led them to his living room, fairly large for a small house, and indicated the mismatched sofas. Ray took an armchair—the last thing he wanted was to risk touching anybody—and kept his gaze away from the others by looking at the furniture while Gabriel rummaged in the kitchen cabinets for something. Back when Gabriel had first moved out, Ray and Josh had expected to be invited to visit, but Gabriel had dismissed the notion as impossible because he'd lived in a studio.

He had moved to this house at some point in the last three years, but he still hadn't asked.

The something turned out to be tequila and glasses, which he deposited in a line on the coffee table and filled up with alcohol as efficiently as any bartender. Ray looked up to meet his eyes when Gabriel picked up a glass and offered it to him. He took it and threw it back, the sting of the tequila felt like the only real thing in the world. He wordlessly put his glass out for more. Gabriel poured it for him. He then looked at the other alphas. "Feel free, gentlemen."

Josh looked doubtful, but Iesu and Sergi went for the liquid courage without hesitation. Sergi must have known Gabriel well enough to feel confident pouring in his house because he didn't hesitate to refill the glasses. Ray set his tumbler in easy reach and pretended not to notice the hesitant glance Sergi shot his way before filling it a third time. He didn't like Tequila—or whatever passed as Tequila in the pack, which they had all been warned would send a human to hospital—but he drank anyway.

"I will go first," Gabriel said. They all turned to look at him. "I'm gay, Ray, and I'm going crazy in this pack. And I always liked you. I would like to offer to be your mate."

"Offer?" Ray repeated, putting the glass down so clumsily he almost broke it. "How is it a fucking offer if it's already been signed off by the First Alpha and the council?"

Gabriel met his eyes from where he was still standing across the room. "I can walk away, if you want me to."

Was it a trick? Ray wondered. Of course Gabriel could say what he liked, but in the end he didn't *have* to do anything.

"We all agreed," Josh said quietly from his left.

Ray took his glass and downed it. "Great, now I get to kick you out if I want, and what? Hope nobody worse comes along?"

"Thomas asked," Josh said, apologetically.

"What?!" Ray spat. "Why would that arsehole..."

And then he understood: Thomas was an arsehole, but he was a power-hungry arsehole. He probably didn't have much interest in Ray, but Ray was the beginning of a new pack. A pack where a First Alpha would eventually emerge. Ray could see what Josh was saying: there were way worse choices than the men in this room.

"I like your paintings," Sergi said, out of the blue. Ray turned his way to find he was looking at his own hands on his lap—not exactly the picture of a domineering alpha—and he spoke quietly, like he was... shy. Sergi, who'd screamed to his face and got into more than one fistfight over the years. "I saw them at school and I tracked you down, but I couldn't... I couldn't tell you. I didn't even know why back then. I thought you were cool and I wanted to be your friend, but I didn't know *how*, and then I threw that ball at you hoping you'd catch it and we could get talking."

It was such a stupid story, but Sergi, for all he was nervous, wasn't lying. Even without being able to detect whether someone was truthful by the little giveaways of their pulse and tone, Ray knew it. Nobody outside of his art lessons and his family knew he painted. Except apparently the boy who'd passed the ball so hard, he'd given Ray a nosebleed. Ray had never lost the conviction that it had been intentional. Now that he knew he had been both completely right and completely wrong, he didn't know what to say.

"But what happened?" It was Iesu. Sergi sent a venomous look his way.

"He gave me a nosebleed," Ray explained, and Iesu snorted and elbowed Sergi.

"Is that your thing with people you like?" he teased and Sergi jostled him right back, looking red-faced and... harmless. He was only a little older than Ray himself, not really old enough to be a grown-up. Not old enough to do *this*. Ray wasn't ready.

Not that he thought he'd ever be ready for his role in this pack, to become their omega, but he definitely wasn't ready now.

Iesu turned to Ray. Iesu's dark eyes weren't skittering away from his nervously like Sergi's had been, and somehow that caught him. "I don't really like the way this pack is run. No offense but..." He shrugged. "It's more like an army than a family. I want something small, like it was when it was just us on our own, when I was a kid."

He wasn't talking about Ray at all. But then again, why would he? Why would he choose Ray? Because he played footie well? Iesu gave him a smile then, coy but not quite. And he went right ahead and lightened up his confession. "And I might have lost that match because I was checking you out in those shorts."

From someone else, a compliment about his body might have been insulting under the circumstances. After all, alphas were always attracted to omegas—no matter what they looked like. But Iesu had found a way around it: he'd spoken of Ray's body from before even a hint of the change had taken place. He'd wanted Ray for his own sake, for no other reason than he was a boy in fine shape during a sweaty football match.

Ray found himself snorting, and aimed a half-hearted glare his way. "You keep telling yourself that if it helps you with the utter humiliation of losing to a team with one player down."

He'd liked Iesu, before, but it didn't change the way his chest felt heavy with dread now at the prospect of what Iesu was asking from him. Ray would have probably taken Iesu up for it if he'd offered, back then. But now—

A glass clinked heavily on the wooden table, interrupting his thoughts. He looked and saw that Alec was staring straight at him, shoulders back and posture stiff. Ray didn't even need a nose to see that he was afraid.

"I know we have never met." Alec told him. The rest were quiet, they had to be because Alec's voice had gone deep and low. He could only keep his golden eyes on Ray for a moment before he had to look away. "But I've got something to offer: I'm a doctor."

Werewolves healed fast, but that brought its own set of problems: bones setting in the wrong position, or wounds that healed before they could be cleaned of gravel. Packs needed doctors, even if all they were trained in was human medicine. And then Ray understood what Alec was too delicate to mention: soon *Ray* would need a doctor. Because he'd be pregnant, and then he—

"Tell him why you want to join us," Gabriel encouraged. Ray was almost grateful for the interruption. He'd take anything over his own thoughts.

"Well, I..." Alec's gaze was down, but then he looked up and met Ray's eyes straight on. It took him visible effort and with his boyish features and long-lashed eyes, he looked so young then. He couldn't be, of course, he had to be in his mid-twenties if he'd graduated from university. "I don't like women," he finally admitted. "I've tried and I can't do it. But my parents aren't going to be patient much longer." He licked his lips. "I don't know what I can offer, other than to care for you. But you can ask. I'm all out of options, and I don't want to leave."

"I..." Ray started, looking among their feet to avoid their eyes, and he had absolutely no idea what to say. Josh—who had witnessed him blanking in front of teachers all his life—knew it and, just like then, he stepped up.

"I'm sure nobody expects an answer right away, Ray," he commented lightly. But he meant it: nobody was going to ask Ray to decide right then and there. "How long does he have before the heat rises?"

"A day, maybe, it... it depends," Alec answered, and Ray didn't need to hear the way his voice had thickened to know what he was feeling. He could *smell it*. The word 'heat' had sent every alpha in the room from low-banked arousal to full hardness, and Ray's own body reacted to that. Except he wasn't hard. No. He was getting *wet*.

Ray's wolf wanted to rumble in satisfaction. Ray wanted the earth to open up and swallow him whole.

Chapter 2

Nobody tried to talk him out of reading magazines in Gabriel's guest room with the door closed. After an hour or so, Josh brought him dinner without asking him to come to the table first. Despite being half-nauseous with terror, Ray discovered he was also starving. He was surprised by how good the food was, and especially at the inclusion of vegetables. He found his dish was clean before he was satisfied. As if he could read his mind, Josh knocked again with another plate. "Alec says you'll want to keep your strength, if you can manage."

Ray kept his eyes firmly on the plate and nodded in thanks. He couldn't manage anything more. Josh left him to it without another word.

The others must have figured out Josh had a way with him. Or maybe because Josh had recruited them, they felt they had to listen to him when it came to Ray. In any case, it was also he who came to get the plates later.

Ray was distracted, looking at some cool glasses that let you watch movies in them, and accidentally looked up at his friend, just in time to catch Josh's pupils dilating. He gasped and got his own faceful of alpha pheromones. Ray quickly looked away, dropping the magazine as a shudder ran through his body like an earthquake, leaving him shaky and out of breath. The only thing he wanted was for Josh to leave so he could relieve the unbearable pressure in his trousers. The fallen magazine was disguising his erection from sight—but he was very aware Josh must have been able to smell it anyway.

But Josh just stood there for a long minute before clearing his throat. "Leaving it to the last minute will make it worse because we won't have time to prepare," he explained. He sounded like he was speaking at gunpoint.

Ray shrugged, words were beyond him now.

"I'll send Alec and Gabriel ahead to find... the place, and then we can go together," Josh continued—so hesitantly that it could have been a question. But it wasn't. They had all offered to leave if he wanted, but it wasn't *them* Ray had a problem with, and he could not leave himself. With maybe only hours left before heat peaked and left him unable to think at all, let alone make any reasonable decisions, it would be utter idiocy to refuse Josh's efforts and try his luck talking to other candidates.

He didn't think he could take the humiliation of interviewing people who saw fucking him as a free ticket to being alpha of a new pack in prime territory. And if he refused Josh himself, he knew very well he'd never be allowed to spend time with him again. Omegas weren't forbidden from talking to unmated alphas, but they couldn't really be friends. Especially not if that alpha had made it clear he was interested in mating them.

When he'd heard his uncle's words, he'd thought he had lost everything. But you could always lose more.

By the time they made it to the clearing, Gabriel and Alec had scouted the territory that was to become theirs; Ray'd gone from overheated to feverish and not even the chilly night was enough to cool him down. Josh had hold of his arm and Ray was leaning on him more than he'd have liked to admit—more for the contact than the support. He was hard in his jeans and dizzy with it. His mind was foggy too, drunk on hormones.

And the alphas around him weren't any better: Nobody except Josh was touching him yet, but they didn't need to for Ray to smell how impatient and eager they were. Their scent made Ray even more desperate for it. He didn't care that Sergi was a bit of a prick, or that he had known Alec for less than half a day, or that Gabriel had probably sung nursery rhymes to him once upon a time. He'd have probably slept with Iesu and Josh before if they'd asked, but he wouldn't have let them lay him down on a blanket like they were doing. He wouldn't have lain there, eyes closed and muscles unwound, as their hands got to his clothes, unlacing and unbuttoning, lifting his hips and making him sit up to pull his shirt off. He wouldn't have nuzzled their hands, trying to keep them touching him because their touch was the only thing that relieved the unbearable heat of his skin.

His knees were lifted and his hole exposed. He was dripping slick already, his body desperate for it. He felt something even hotter nudge between his legs at the place where he felt so empty. Then the cock was going into him, opening him up, slow but still feeling too big for that small space in Ray's body. Ray's hips twisted of their own accord, trying to adjust, but the alpha didn't stop. He didn't slam into

Ray, just move slow and steady as if he knew it was the right thing to do until finally Ray felt his pubic hair rubbing ticklishly against his exposed balls.

He opened his eyes. It was Gabriel. He smiled approvingly and hooked Ray's legs over his own shoulders. "There you go, sweetheart, you're being so good."

Ray blinked heavily at him, unable to process, and Gabriel pulled out and moved back into him. He was huge and it felt like he was dragging Ray's insides with him when he withdrew—inside him, though, the wolf howled with joy. And he was hard, his cock red and dripping against his own stomach, twitching with each speeding thrust. He didn't know when it went from painful to uncomfortable and from uncomfortable to good. But then it became too much, and Gabriel was hitting just the right angle to set Ray's insides alight. Ray wanted to touch himself, but his hands wouldn't move where they lay on the thin blanket, fingertips so sensitive he could feel the grass underneath. All he could do was cry out as his cousin rammed into him and set the reaction off again, too much and never enough. He wanted... No, he *needed*— He glanced around, seeking...

The others were all watching, two on each side, all of them with visible bulges in their trousers, and Ray could *smell them*. Smell how much they wanted him, what they would do to him. Gabriel rocked him with an especially powerful thrust of his hips and Ray whined low in his throat, not sure if it hurt because his cousin had broken something in him or because his release was so near and yet he couldn't reach it. Then Gabriel was leaning forward and taking hold of Ray's hair, pulling his head to the side to expose his throat and setting his sharp teeth deep into Ray's skin. The cock inside Ray pulsed and Gabriel was coming, wet and slick into Ray's already slick hole. And just like that, Ray seemed to be free to orgasm himself. It hit him like a freight train, vision exploding with light as his whole body sang with it.

When he was conscious of his body again, it was because his arse was getting fuller still. Gabriel hadn't pulled out and now he was knotting—the head of his cock expanding to keep his seed from leaving the deeper passages of Ray's body. Knotting wasn't necessary but it ensured conception. It also *hurt*. He tossed his head, whining, unable to find the words to complain. Gabriel rubbed his face, soothing him with whispered endearments when Ray just needed him to *pull out*. But he couldn't, and he didn't.

When Gabriel did withdraw, the pressure eased as come dripped out of Ray's hole. The relief was so intense that Ray went easily when he was guided to his hands and knees, arms and legs shaking with the effort of not falling down face-first. Not all of it had had time to come out when they filled him again. He didn't know if it was bigger or he was just sore, but he shivered, involuntarily clenching against the invasion. Then there were arms holding him close against the body on top of him and next to his ear a familiar voice was whispering. "Shh, it's okay, Ray. I got you now. I'm sorry I couldn't go first," Josh was saying.

Ray froze with the knowledge: *Josh was inside him.*

He struggled a little more—not with Josh, who he could have shaken, but with his wolf, who was in control during heat—and Josh's hold tightened.

"Does it hurt?" he whispered and he sounded like he was in pain himself. Ray closed his eyes, giving in, and his wolf surged to the surface, stronger during the full moon than it ever was when Ray was in human shape. His hips wiggled under Josh, *around* Josh, clenching now with intent because the wolf *wanted* to be mounted. No, it *needed* it. Josh let out a choked sound above him and his hips snapped a quick thrust in response. He moaned Ray's name, sounding broken. "Ray, I can't... I need..." He was almost sobbing as he fucked into Ray's body, faster and harder as the heat took hold of him, as instinct led him to fulfil his deepest desires and take the omega that was his.

Later, all Ray remembered the second knotting hadn't hurt as much as the first, and he Josh's gentle hands as he laid him on his back afterwards and took his mouth into a soft kiss Ray didn't have the energy to return. He thought it'd been Sergi next, but he wasn't sure. He let his eyes fall closed even as his legs were lifted once again and then there was the newly familiar feeling of being penetrated, now through the seed of two alphas as well as his own juices. It went in easy, and then it went in again. At some point, he found he wasn't on his back anymore but had his face pressed against the blanket instead—it smelled of sweat and come now, not grass—and his arse was in the air, another cock moving rhythmically inside him. The discomfort of knottings was a vague recollection, the bites nothing but a sting in his hazy state. He closed his eyes as one alpha after another came and used him, again and again as if they'd never be sated.

Chapter 3

Gabriel wanted to keep Ray in his house while they built the first house in the new territory. The five alphas of the pack had been freed from their usual work in their current pack to complete the house as soon as possible. Iesu, though, didn't see why Ray couldn't spend some time with each of them instead. Neither Alec nor Sergi had commented yet when Josh interrupted the squabble with more authority than Ray had believed him capable of.

"I think we should ask Ray what he wants. His mother would probably be happy to see him, for one thing."

"Yes," Gabriel rapidly agreed. From where he was sprawled on the sofa with the remote, Ray thought he looked genuinely contrite. "Of course. Sorry, Ray," he told him then. "Just..." He licked his lips. "I really want to keep an eye on you, I guess," he explained wryly.

Of course, it was hard to tell what anybody was feeling when you couldn't look them in the eyes, and Ray felt so numb inside he thought he might be unable to *recognize* emotions. But if there was one thing he wanted, it was to be left alone. And he loved his mother and his siblings, but they would be all over him, concerned and caring and overwhelming.

And she would know. She knew now, of course. Ray had no illusions that the whole pack wasn't aware, but the possibility that she might *talk* about it... He couldn't bear it. It wasn't her fault; there was nothing she could have done differently once he'd presented omega. But he didn't want her comfort now, her empty promises; not when he now knew the truth of his situation so intimately.

It hadn't been a lie, he'd wanted them all, hadn't even cared who was taking a turn mounting him, and the knowledge filled him with shame. This was all he was: an animal, full of need and instinct and ready to let any alpha have him. Except not any alpha, not anymore; they hadn't just bred him, they'd bitten him. A mate bite to mark he belonged to them, the marks were bruises in the shapes of their teeth around his neck and back, visible to all and sure to scar.

"I'll stay. You guys should go get the materials," he said, trying for his most reasonable voice. Still, he mostly sounded tired. He saw Josh's shoes take a step closer to him, but then Gabriel's voice was booming out.

"Come on, guys, you heard him. Let's get to work on the new house!" He then proceeded to hustle them out of the house. Before leaving he turned and shouted at Ray, "Keys are by the fruit bowl!"

Like Ray had any intention of going anywhere. As soon as the sounds of... his pack went away, Ray turned off the TV and pulled the blanket down to cover his face. The fantasy worlds of faraway lives made for a good distraction when the others were around, but now that he was finally alone, he wanted real oblivion.

His memories of that night a week ago when his pack had taken him to their new territory and claimed it by claiming Ray weren't easy to drown out. And any time he remembered, Ray flushed with both shame and remembered desire. There should have been nothing like that. He'd desired men before, but he'd never wanted to be *taken*. And that was without even thinking about what was happening inside him now... He twisted, trying to get his long frame comfortable on the rather small couch that had probably come with the flat. He buried his face in the cushions, but they smelled of the alphas and there was no way to think of them without thinking about what Ray had let them do to him. It was happening already, even if he could only feel it so faintly he thought he might be imagining it.

His body was already changing, and it was too late to do anything about it. He wasn't imagining it: inside him, they were growing.

It was Josh who woke him up for dinner, slow and careful. The others were in the house, too, Ray could hear the bustle of cooking and cutlery coming from Gabriel's overpopulated kitchen. But it had taken Josh carefully shaking his shoulder to wake him.

"Whattimeitis?" Ray mumbled, trying to swallow the bad taste off his mouth.

"Ten," Josh replied. "We got the ground levelled," he added, and Ray nodded. He had lived with builders all his life, but he didn't really know what half of their conversations were about.

They were lucky Gabriel was an expert and could handle a one level building without them needing to pay anybody—either in cash or favours.

"Ray, I..." his friend started. Josh's hand was still on his arm. He could feel the pressure on his arm, but it was like he had to look to actually understand it was happening, as if his skin had refused to alert his brain. "Are you... I mean, do you think you'll be okay? Is there anything I can do to make you be okay?"

You could not have fucked me on the ground with your new pack, Ray thought resentfully. Then he regretted it; once an omega presented there was nothing that could prevent his heat and the longer a heat was left unattended, the more dangerous it became. The omega's body would go into shock in the same way any body did when not provided what it needed. And Josh had been gentle, and he was looking after Ray now, trying to see not just to his physical needs but to still be his friend. It was just that Ray didn't know *how*. It had been a whole eight days and he still couldn't look at Josh without thinking about the weight of his body, of his...

And if he managed to forget that, then the way his senses had heightened even further since the heat reminded him of what else Josh had done to him. He shrugged. "I... I just want to be alone."

Josh hesitated, then squeezed his arm. "Okay, dinner will be ready in a minute and then you can hole up in Gabriel's spare room."

Dinner was too loud in the small living room, and Ray felt too warm even though they had left an armchair all for him while they shared the couch and a chair that didn't seem like it could support anybody's weight. More than once something almost fell from the coffee table, which was definitely not designed for six people to eat a proper meal on, much less six grown werewolves.

But the alphas didn't touch Ray, and they didn't speak directly to him. He could let their voices wash over him, not hearing their words, not even following who was speaking. The wolf was quiet inside him, knowing it was safe surrounded by his alphas, and that was all Ray could ask for.

I t was normally Josh corralling Ray after dinner to try and get him to take a walk, or talk about his day or generally open up. But the night after that, it was Alec. Ray stared at him in surprise when he asked if Ray would take a walk with him. Ray didn't want to, of course, but the wolf jumped at the chance of pleasing his alpha. Plus, Alec looked so discomfited to be asking for anything that he had to believe it was important.

He was as nervous as ever, if not more. "Ray, do you... I don't really know what you prefer so I'm going to have to take your word for it."

"Okay," Ray said. It seemed like a safe response when he had no idea what Alec was talking about.

Alec paused and Ray could feel the weight of his gaze on his own face even as he carefully stared into the distance. It was a beautiful night, bright and starry and with a leftover hint of pink among the dark blue. "Do you want me to be direct with you about medical matters?"

"Direct?" Ray echoed. Then hesitated. "What's the other option?"

Alec looked away, licking his lips, then offered, "Analogies."

There was only one reason to ask something like that: it wasn't good news. But Ray was a ripping-plasters-off kind of guy.

"Just tell me," he said. "The sooner I know, the sooner I can decide to jump off a cliff." Alec's pause was long enough to make Ray nervous. "What?" he demanded. "Is it really that bad?"

"No!" Alec assured him. "Um, at least, I hope not."

Ray rolled his eyes at him. He wondered if Alec was always like this or if it was being around an omega that had fried his brain. "Didn't you just say you were gonna be direct?"

"Yes! And I will," Alec said, then his lips kept moving but no words were coming out. Just when Ray was about to snap at him again, he blurted it out, "We are not going to be able to stay away for much longer."

"Stay away?"

"From you. From... your bed."

Ray massaged the bridge of his nose, mostly to hide his face from the other man. "Because you don't have to."

"No!" Alec sounded horrified at the suggestion. "It's the instincts, an alpha needs his claimed omega to smell like him, to... and the..." He swallowed audibly. "...the babies make it worse."

"Worse?" Ray asked when he could swallow past the lump in his throat. *The babies.* He'd known. Of course he'd known, he'd been in heat and he'd been knotted by five alphas, there had never been any chance that he wasn't... But it wasn't the same. He was already feeling sick at the idea, or possibly it was a side effect of the fact itself... and it wouldn't even help keep the alphas happy? "Not better?"

After all, now he had no choice, he couldn't go anywhere, not even if he wanted to. They had planted a part of themselves in him that tied him to them forever. They would take over his body, changing him into something they could use.

But even without those dark thoughts, it was a fact: if surviving on his own had been unlikely, surviving with a bunch of babies was downright impossible. And what more guarantee could the alphas need that nobody was going to steal him away? They'd claimed him and they'd marked him and they'd made him into *this*. He was shaking with anger at the sheer injustice, at how *much* was being asked of him, and how much more there was left to ask when he felt like he had nothing left to give.

Alec took a step back, sensing his anger. "I'm sorry, it does make it better. If you weren't... We'd not have been able to resist this long. It's only the instinct to protect you that's kept the wolves at bay. But... it's not enough."

Ray put a hand up against the side of the house to keep himself upright. "Why are you telling me this?"

"Because you deserve the truth," Alec said earnestly.

"But why tell me now?" Ray insisted. There was no point in knowing if there was nothing he could do to avoid it.

"There's... some flexibility. You can control the timing, to an extent. Except for the next full moon."

Ray closed his eyes at the onslaught of memories the mention of the goddess brought with it. He had thought... he'd thought that since he wouldn't go into heat during the next full moon, he'd be safe. "You are saying I have *to ask for it* or next full moon you will all... it will all happen again?"

"I don't know if we'll make it two more weeks, Ray," Alec said quietly, ashamed.

"I can't *ask* for it!" The words felt like they were torn out of his throat. "You can't expect... I *can't.*"

Alec hesitated. "But it's what you need, to be safe," he said. Ray didn't think it he was explaining it to Ray, just confirming it. He didn't object. It sounded like he didn't have a choice about it, once again, and so what if Alec wanted to tell himself Ray 'needed' the least terrible option he had? He could believe what he wanted; it wouldn't make Ray's life less fucked up.

"I have to..." Ray said vaguely and turned around to walk back inside.

Alec didn't try to follow, but Ray thought he heard him say something just when the front door opened to let out Sergi and Iesu. Ray quickly tore his eyes away from their startled faces and they paused only a moment before moving out of his way.

Chapter 4

It was Josh who came to him first, naturally. Gabriel had been bringing him fruit and he'd offered to drive him to his mother's—as if he couldn't walk, but Ray understood his cousin had little more to offer. But it was Josh who still felt confident enough to try and help, even when there wasn't anything he could do that would really make things any better. It was like Josh was holding his hand as he died, or offering sips of water as fever ravaged his body, barely managing to bring him any relief at all.

But the fact that he was trying was in itself a comfort and Ray knew it must have cost him. When Josh sat with him in a darkened room and rearranged his blankets and forced him to have a drink, Ray wondered what he'd have felt if he'd been the one on the other side. It made him cringe to think of Josh on the ground instead, of watching as the others took turns. He'd have wanted to look away and he wouldn't have been able to. An alpha wouldn't have been able to look away from an omega in the middle of heat, even if the man inside the wolf wanted to more than anything.

Gabriel probably hadn't wanted to be the one to have the conversation with Ray—he'd always been a cheerful guy, refusing to dwell on problems, distracting everybody with a joke or a game or ice-cream. That was the only reason Ray could think that Alec had been sent to tell him. Alec was a doctor, sure, but it wasn't like that meant he understood their instincts better. Werewolves didn't really believe in doctors for themselves; nobody could tell Ray why he had presented omega and according to Alec, they couldn't predict the frequency of his heats either. And so of course now it would be Josh to come and see him, because Ray knew all the facts and what he needed the most was comfort, support, and even Gabriel must have known there was no cheering him up in these circumstances. He wouldn't have wanted to fail, so he'd let someone else do it.

"Hey," his friend greeted and his voice gave away what his scent didn't: he didn't want to be here. He didn't want to see Ray like this.

"Hey," Ray said back, keeping his eyes on the laptop where he was aimlessly browsing landscapes.

"Did Alec... he said he talked to you," Josh prompted. But Ray wasn't any readier to talk about it now than he had been before. He didn't move. "Fuck, Ray, I don't... How am I supposed to know how to help you if you won't talk to me?"

"Talk to Alec, I'm guessing," Ray said evenly. He expanded the picture of the desert to see if it was a snake in the corner. Could one hallucinate in the desert without the heat, just because everything looked the same? He wondered, squinting at the darkness in the corner that was looking less like a snake every minute...

Josh didn't react to the snark. Instead he got closer and sat on the bed next to Ray. Ray tensed, he couldn't help it—but he didn't look at him. Not even when Josh's hand cupped the elbow closest to him—just like he'd done in the hall—and his thumb started caressing the bare skin there. Ray didn't move, except to click on another image. He had no idea what the image was—with Josh there, so close, all he could feel was the growing tightness in his trousers. The laptop would hide it, though. Whatever his traitorous body thought, Ray didn't want to get bent over and stuffed with cock. Josh's fingers slowly curled around his triceps and Ray had to concentrate to repress a shiver—Josh's hand was hot and his fingertips were newly callused from the construction work. And he smelled... he was hard, and he wanted Ray, not as badly as during heat, but just as truly.

Ray was quiet, and Josh followed his lead, leaning in to nuzzle his throat. He slid his hand from Ray's arm onto his side as his tongue darted out to lick the mark his teeth had left on the side of Ray's neck. Ray shuddered, and, to make up for it, clicked another link. The laptop was heavy and too warm on his straining cock now, but he *wouldn't*. He didn't want this. Josh's hand found its way under his T-shirt and his touch made Ray struggle to stay still. Josh must have noticed both the forced immobility and the scent of arousal, he was too close to miss it; but he didn't say anything or even pause. He took the laptop off Ray's hands like he might have removed a bottle if he was drunk, methodical but gentle. And when Ray's lap was exposed, he just lowered his hands to flick the button of Ray's pants open and lower the zip.

Controlling his breathing was a lost cause now that Ray didn't have the computer to focus on. He gave in and closed his eyes as Josh's hands began exploring him. He didn't know how to stop himself from being turned on: Josh just smelled so good, and he was touching him so softly and not shying away from where—had he been able to speak—Ray might have asked him to put his hands. He handled Ray's hard cock like it was a fine piece of machinery, grip tight but careful with his nails and, without meaning to, Ray found his hips rising to follow the movement. He clenched to push up and froze, whimpering in frustration and pleasure both as he felt the slickness already coating his insides. The sensation sent a thrilling rush through him directly to his cock and made him want to throw himself off the bed. Josh had to hold him down as he arched higher and started to come, trembling all over, getting it on Josh's hand and arm and probably all over the bed, too.

He fell back down panting madly, staring at the inside of his own eyelids. He had never come that fast before, not even when he was just starting to jerk off. When he felt Josh's hands leave him, probably to clean up, he allowed himself to relax. A moment later, he almost fell off the bed when his friend leaned close and licked his hipbone. Ray looked down, unable to believe it, and his eyes met Josh's looking right up at him and licking his lips clean of Ray's come. Without looking away, Josh leaned back in and licked again, collecting more of Ray's come with his curved tongue and swallowing it with evident pleasure. Ray couldn't look away from his mouth. His spent cock twitched and he could feel himself getting wetter, the slick pooling under him. Josh's next lick made him squirm and by the next he needed to fist his hands on the bed to keep himself from touching. He couldn't hold back the sounds, though, and that hurt, too, the admission. By the time Josh finished cleaning him up, Ray was a shivering mess and his cock was half hard again, still sensitive from coming and from all the attention, but also...

"That helps," Josh said, breaking the silence like he had been keeping silent simply because he had nothing to say. His next words belied the apparent carelessness. His voice was rough, but still only a whisper, "I need to come now, but you don't need to do anything, just stay there."

He straddled Ray's lap and opened up his own zip with a half bitten off moan, then took hold of his cock and started stripping it so fast his hand blurred. Ray shifted under him, feeling the wetness inside him and wanting... And Josh started coming, just because Ray had *moved*. Ray barely had time to close his eyes before he was covered in it, his chin and lips as well as his whole chest marked by seed.

Josh was panting harshly over him, but after a moment Ray felt him shift and realised he was using his own shirt to clean up. He was careful around his eyes, even though Ray could feel him shaking, but Ray didn't open them again. He could smell Josh on him now and it quieted something in him. No, something in the wolf—Ray's own head was filled with noise and the sound of Josh's voice—soft as it was—only added to his confusion.

"I'll tell him to be quiet," Josh murmured, "but it's better to get it over with, isn't it? And it'll feel good now."

Ray turned his head, containing his instinctive flinch and unable to control his blush—it would feel good, Josh meant, because Ray was gagging for it, so ready that Josh must have smelled him. His friend paused for a moment longer, but he didn't say anything more. Not even who he meant.

Not that it really mattered; Alec had made it quite clear that each member of the pack would be visiting Ray's bed in the near future.

His orgasm had relaxed him enough that he was drifting by the time the door opened again. He was immediately alert in the presence of an alpha, but he didn't open his eyes. The alpha had to have known he was awake—it was impossible to miss the accelerated rhythm of his heartbeat. But Ray didn't care. He just wanted to be able to pretend, not to have to be here, as much as he could not be here, when it happened.

And maybe it was also intended as a kindness when he was quickly turned over onto his front and his jeans were yanked only as low as was necessary to expose his arse. There was a muffled groan. Ray didn't quite manage not to tense when he imagined the sight he must present, soaked as he was. But the hands continued efficiently and soon the sounds of clothing being shifted were over and the hot skin of an erection was being pressed between his cheeks, kept close by the trousers trapping his thighs together. As wet as he was, the position made it a bit of a struggle to push the member into his hole. He could feel every millimetre as it entered, almost in sync with the heavy breaths puffing against the back of his neck. And then with a final shove that had him clenching, it slid in all the way and the alpha on top of him pressed his chest against Ray's back.

He was heavy on top of Ray, but that didn't tell him much, he'd never had a man's full weight on him for more than a few moments during a fight—not outside of the blurry madness of heat—and his thoughts were too scattered for him to process anything as complex as scent. The wolf knew it was his alpha and that was all it mattered. It didn't make a difference which.

Ray tried to let the wolf win, take over, be the one in the moment, but he couldn't really escape the pleasure his body was drowning him in, each thrust sending waves of desire higher and higher until it was all he could manage to stay still under the man mounting him. His own cock was trapped under him into the half twisted covers, sliding into the mess of come and slick he'd produced for Josh, and even if he'd wanted to move, he couldn't have reached it. His lover was pumping his hips hard, faster and harder, clearly pursuing his own release and all Ray could do was take it, fists clenched on the sheets and body burning. And then he was being crushed by even more weight, his breath knocked out of his lungs even as he turned his face to try and get his mouth out of the bedding and catch some much-needed air. He was vaguely aware of the liquid being pumped into his arse and the sounds of the man on top of him as he reached orgasm. He came as well, either because the alpha wanted it of him or because the last heavy thrusts had overstimulated his prostate until he could do nothing else. But it was the removal of the weight and the sudden ability to inhale again that he remembered more clearly. He kept his eyes closed as his lover petted his waist, pressing close to his side, sticky warm and panting still.

It seemed to take a long time, but then the warm body next to him rolled over and left the bed.

A knock woke him up the next morning and he groaned. His legs were tangled in his twisted bedsheets, one still half-encased in his ruined jeans and his shirt was sticking damply to his skin. He didn't think he'd made any sounds of distress, but the door opened and Alec walked in, asking already if he was okay. Ray scrambled to cover himself, then felt like an idiot: Alec had more than *seen* him naked.

"Did you sleep on your clothes?" the guy asked, surprised. Ray had managed to drag one of the pillows onto his lap but his leg was exposed still. He was a mess and he smelled even worse, of his own come and the alphas'. He shrugged, carefully avoiding looking at Alec. "Are you hungry?" the man continued. "I'll run you a shower and make some breakfast while you get cleaned up," he decided, apparently not requiring any input from Ray himself.

Ray didn't object; he was desperate to be clean and he was starving. He was always starving now. For a moment, he wondered if Alec could explain to him exactly why that was... but the possible answers were all too disturbing. It was one of those times when no good answers existed. He had a shower, scrubbing himself fast and using too much of the vanilla soap, as if chemicals could disguise the scent of his alphas on his skin. And then he went downstairs and ate the bacon, eggs, and beans Alec had made for him. It was a little crispier than he liked—not that he could really taste it, because once he'd put some food into his mouth, he hadn't been able to stop until he'd cleared the plate.

"Damn, but you are hungry."

He nodded, shrugged it off. "Did you make more?"

"Oh, um, yeah, just a sec." Alec practically shot to his feet in eagerness and a moment later he was returning with new plate filled to the brim.

When he simply swapped the plates, Ray gave him a confused look. "I'm not going to die if I have to wait two seconds for you to take my plate to the kitchen, you know?"

Alec actually blushed. With skin as pale as his, it showed easily. "I'm sorry, I just feel... I'm grateful, and I know you're having a hard time of it," he admitted, looking away. "And I feel awful about leaving you to sleep like that."

Ray's fork slipped from his fingers. Now he knew. And suddenly he wanted to get out of the room, he couldn't bear... He hesitated, then got to his feet.

"Thanks for the food," he managed and took the plate back upstairs.

"Ray..." Alec said quietly, but it was quiet enough that Ray could ignore it. It wasn't an order anyway, so he didn't have to stop. He'd get ordered around enough as it was without wasting time and energy he didn't have doing what the alphas wanted when they didn't say what it was.

R ay shot down Josh's attempt to talk him into going out to dinner with them before he could even specify the restaurant. "Forget it," he snapped as soon as his friend mentioned dinner.

Josh didn't push, instead he asked, "Was... Is there anything I can do better?"

Ray almost told him to tell Alec there was no point in fucking Ray in complete silence if he then went and told him he had done it the morning after. But *talking* about it would fully defeat the point of Josh's method. "Just want to be alone," he said for what felt like the millionth time.

Josh didn't object, just asked, "Do you want pizza or Chinese?"

"Chinese," Ray decided. "Number 155 and 55. And prawn toast."

"Wow, you—" Josh cut himself off, and there was yet another subject they couldn't really talk about freely anymore.

"I could eat a cow," Ray said, trying to salvage the situation.

Josh bravely followed his lead. "I think you mean a *deer*."

And Ray couldn't look at him, not yet, but he snorted a little laugh.

There were another two alphas that night, but they let him keep his eyes closed and didn't try to talk to him. The first rubbed their cocks together as he bit into Ray's marked-up neck and Ray thought he'd come like that. But as his thrusting got more frantic, there was a muffled sound of frustration against his throat and then his left leg was lifted and he was speared in a sharp shove. He'd buckled, shocked and hurt, clenching around the sudden intrusion and the alpha had started coming, making Ray climax too.

He'd been almost grateful to be put on his hands and knees next and mounted slow and easy, no pretence and no hope, just an efficient fuck—dick swelling inside him and discharging until his thighs were drenched in his own fluid and theirs.

And then he'd been allowed to rest.

The next day Sergi showed up with Ray's art supplies and two new canvases.

"I hope they're the right type," he offered from the doorway of Gabriel's guest room, like a wolf at another's den. "I asked at the shop what was best for oils."

Ray stared at his box of tools, then looked up at Sergi—who had been an arsehole to him plenty, but who at least had the decency not to bring up the previous night's activities directly—and felt a surge of gratitude. Then he realised something else. "Did you see them?"

He didn't say who he meant, but Sergi got it in one. "See them? Your mother made me stay for lunch and give her an update! She's worried sick, but she doesn't want to walk into your territory when you don't even have a territory yet."

Ray's stomach twisted—he'd been so busy feeling sorry for himself it hadn't even occurred to him that his mother was now effectively a member of another pack and couldn't simply visit him when she pleased. The first omega of a pack felt the land their pack occupied as intensely theirs, the most skilled of them could tell where any wolf—their own or foreign—was at any given time. But Ray didn't really have a territory. Even though they'd christened the ground that first night of his heat, he wouldn't be able to feel it until he was actually there. He could tell if there was someone in the house, but not who, and he hadn't even considered that it could be something beyond the advanced hearing and smelling abilities he'd had his whole life.

He didn't think he would have minded if another omega had walked into Gabriel's house, but he wasn't sure he wanted to see his mother there, either.

"What did you tell her?" he asked Sergi.

Sergi shrugged, the same air of superiority that irritated Ray about him now seemed simply self-confidence. "The truth: that you are bored." He tapped the case of brushes meaningfully, eyes following his own fingers. "And lonely and freaked out," he added in the exact same tone, like he was doing nothing but listing the facts.

Ray knew how very capable he was of twisting words into ugliness, and now suddenly he discovered that he was equally good at the opposite. He could turn a description of Ray's life—the disaster that was Ray's life—into nothing more than incidental discomfort. It should have been galling, but Sergi wasn't dismissing Ray's pain—he'd gone and done his best to solve two out of the three problems he'd listed—and Ray could hear he was sincere. He *believed it* when he added, "But that with a little time, you'll be fine. And then you'll call her and of course she and your siblings will be welcome in our territory any time."

Ray wasn't so sure. He didn't think he'd ever be okay again, that he would ever be able to be himself again. "You seem very sure of that," he said. He wasn't angry at Sergi for being confident, not really, but...

Sergi met his eyes now that Ray was looking. He was actually ridiculously handsome when he wasn't sneering. His skin was a little darker than Iesu's, and a warmer shade too, closer to chocolate than copper, while his eyes were a light hazel. It would have been pretty hard to choose between one set of lush dark eyelashes and the other. It was stunning on them both, but while Iesu would bat his and flirt, Sergi's serious expression made being watched by him an almost physical experience. Ray looked away, fixing his gaze on the supplies. It wasn't a good thought to have at the moment.

"I spent a lot of time fighting with you," Sergi said. "I figure I know what you're made of by now."

Ray hesitated, then said, "Thanks for the supplies."

Sergi didn't linger, just nodded and headed out, probably back to the construction site. Of all the alphas in his pack, it was Sergi that had worried Ray the most, and he was—besides Josh—turning out to be the sweetest, not just concerning himself with Ray's welfare but looking after his family as well.

But it wasn't like Ray could do something for him. If what Ray was doing wasn't enough, it was simply because there wasn't enough in him to be a good omega.

"Open your eyes, Ray," Gabriel ordered as soon as he sat down next to him on the bed. And Ray did. It was a direct order from his alpha. His cousin leaned close and cupped his face, looking into his eyes until Ray looked away. He was trembling and ashamed of it, but he thought that if Gabriel made him look him in the eye, he'd cry. "I thought you were just overwhelmed during heat," Gabriel said thoughtfully. "Have you been doing this with the others?" Ray didn't answer, but Gabriel seemed to know anyway. His hand was on Ray's hair, which was too long now by half, but shorter than Gabriel's still. "I know it's a lot to take in," he said. "But you can't shut yourself off from your whole life."

He waited for a moment, then he asked, "What do you want to do?" And when Ray didn't reply, he imbued some power into his voice. "Tell me."

Ray tried to resist for a moment, gritting his teeth, but in the end, it was pointless. "I want to be alone."

Gabriel's hand ceased its caresses. "Okay, that was stupid. I'm sorry you're not ready, but I can't keep my wolf under control anymore. I need to have sex with you now. Just tell me what will make it less uncomfortable for you."

It was so fucking reasonable, but Ray's jaw was locked—he couldn't quite tell if it was fury or terror or sheer stubbornness—and then Gabriel sighed and he ordered, once again, "Tell me."

"I don't want to talk about it."

"What?" he asked, looking sincerely puzzled.

Ray swallowed thickly, then sat up, realising Gabriel hadn't ordered him to lie down. Not yet. "You need to do it. I need not to think about it." He glared. None of the others had insisted like this, and why should they? They could take what they needed, and Ray could do his best to survive it.

Gabriel hesitated a moment longer, "Okay, but this can't go on. You need... We'll work on it."

Ray didn't respond, he didn't have a choice either way, so why argue? When he closed his eyes and reclined back down, Gabriel didn't object. By the time he opened Ray's zip and lowered his underwear, Ray was wet for him. Gabriel hummed his approval, but didn't speak. He turned him over and pushed his shoulders down against the bedding, pulling on his hips to raise his arse. Ray could feel Gabriel's heavy cock brushing against his balls—heavy and swollen—as his alpha shifted his hips to try to slot himself in. Ray squirmed, unable to take the teasing. It wasn't as bad as talking, but his body's betrayal burned nonetheless.

And then Gabriel betrayed him, too. "Oh, you want it," he murmured, wonderingly.

Ray wanted to hit him. It was such a stupid thing to say: an omega was always ready for his alpha. Ray had actually less choice about being aroused than about continuing to breathe. But alphas liked to think an omega getting wet meant they were into it, that they wanted to be used.

It was even hard for Ray to tell if anything of what he was feeling came from himself. His hole was clenching desperately and when Gabriel finally popped the head in, the relief was so intense his elbows buckled, sending him face-first into the pillow for a long breathless moment. Once into the slick passage, there wasn't much to keep Gabriel's cock from sliding all the way in, and when the huge thing pushed against Ray's prostate, his hips twisted of their own accord, opening him up to it. Gabriel groaned on top of him. He was holding onto Ray's hips, and with a languorous, slow twist of his cock inside Ray, he pulled out and pushed back in fast, pulling and pushing on Ray's hips to fuck him onto his cock. Ray let him, concentrating on keeping his mouth free of any bedding so he could breathe through it all. At least Gabriel was quiet, no more sex talk and no questions. And after he was done, he went and got a towel and wiped the mess off Ray before covering him up.

When he woke up, Ray could almost pretend he was a little sore from exercise and that he had sweated in his sleep because summer was coming up. There was only cereal and fruit for breakfast, but he'd take it.

Chapter 5

He had expected to leave the supplies—thoughtful as they were—languishing in a corner of the guest room. But he didn't really have much to do: he'd stopped going to college when he'd presented, and other than Josh, he wasn't talking to any of his old friends. There wasn't any point: In a few months, he wouldn't be able to see them anyway, and after that he'd be too busy with the pack for humans.

Television and the internet had kept him sufficiently distracted so far, but he still found himself sketching in bed the very next day. Not just doodling but trying out angles and shading with the two canvases Sergi had brought in mind. After years of hard labour—between his siblings, school, hunting and whatever else the pack needed—the notion of being home all day doing nothing was unbearable. He could have cooked or cleaned, but nobody had really brought it up and the last thing he wanted were more omega responsibilities. So he put some music on and kept it up, taking a break to make himself a sandwich for lunch. Then, when he was feeling as empty of turmoil as he thought he was going to manage with the power of art, he picked up the phone and called his mother.

"Ray!" Her voice was weak with relief, a tone that had often come up when one of her five kids had shown after a scrape or an unexpectedly long absence. Often it preceded the shouting and a hell of a grounding, but that, at least, was a problem of the past. Not that Ray often got in trouble, not when he'd spent sleepless nights himself waiting for one of his younger siblings. He understood why she needed to know; he just couldn't bear the idea of telling her.

"Hi, mum."

"Are you okay? You sound... your— your alpha said you were okay. He's nice, but..."

"I'm okay," Ray said shortly. He couldn't seem to manage to take a breath deep enough to say much more.

But she didn't need him to say much. She was his mother and even on the phone, she could tell. "It'll get better, you have to believe me," she pleaded. "It'll be... odd at the beginning, but you'll grow to like it."

Ray was silent. Did she understand that he did not have a mate like she had? A man who loved him and who was his partner in life? What he had instead were five men to whom he belonged, and who felt they had every right to take what they wanted from him. Men who had been given the mission of breeding a pack out of Ray's body and to whom Ray had to give what his body could produce.

His mother couldn't understand that. Ray remembered his dad, a sweet if gruff man who'd carried him around on his shoulders and often shown up with flowers or little gifts. He'd treated his mother like a queen, not like she was a warm body to— He shook his head, realising he'd stopped listening and he was being asked something. "What?"

The pause was long enough that he knew it had been a serious question. "Do you want to come over for dinner? I bet you are all eating take-away every day," she said reprovingly.

"It can't be healthy for..." she trailed off, but they both knew what she'd been going to say. It couldn't be good for the babies, because of course that's what everybody cared about now. Ray himself was secondary to his function, to his *purpose*.

"I don't think so, I'm... I'm tired, and I'm painting during the day so..."

"Ray, you know I was surprised by all this, but you don't have to be alone with it. I can teach you..."

"Stop!" he snapped, and immediately regretted it. He'd never spoken to his mother like that in his life—not even when he'd been a bratty teen.

"I'm sorry," she said instead of getting angry, and Ray's stomach sank with the heavy weight of guilt.

"No, I didn't mean to shout. It's just... you think it's the same as you and Dad, and it couldn't be more different."

She wasn't deterred. "Maybe it hasn't started the same, but a mate is a mate. You'll feel it soon."

Ray swallowed. A mate was a mate, but he didn't have a mate, he had five. And that also meant he was more likely carrying five babies. It had only been two weeks and his balance was already off, forcing him to readjust to stay upright in the shower and just making him feel... odd. Nothing concrete, just odd.

"Okay," he said, just so he could hang up. Maybe it had been a bad idea to call, but now at least he didn't need to feel guilty. He had done the right thing, and he'd paid for it, just like with everything else. Just like he'd done when he hadn't run away at the first signs of his unexpected presentation.

That night nobody covered him. Instead he stayed up late doing the background of the first painting and heard Gabriel's alarm go off in the other room. A little bit later he heard the sounds of Josh's Jeep—a presentation gift from his grandfather—in the driveway, and soon after the front door closing. Only when he was alone did he dare lie down to sleep. It was stupid, really, to imagine that if he was awake, they wouldn't come.

I t took him a few days to understand it wasn't going to happen every night. The truth was, there was nothing stopping them. Nothing but some protective instincts that only seemed to partially work—covering Ray's physical health but indifferent to his emotional needs. That and common decency. He didn't think they were bad guys. As far as he could tell Josh had been right; they were decent. But they didn't need to be bad; they owned Ray, and there wasn't a good way to possess someone. At least not someone who hadn't grown up expecting to become an omega.

Maybe it was different if you knew, if you thought of it as being protected and cared for—that's how Ray had thought about it when he imagined having an omega of his own. Or maybe his mum was right, maybe it'd come to him. Maybe he'd start to feel better about the sex—which was unarguably spectacular—and the careful treatment, which was intended as a kindness and made him want to push them away. But why? He needed the kindness and they needed the sex; was it really such a bad exchange?

He still didn't sleep well, even though he no longer felt out of place in his cousin's guest room. He could never rid himself of the sensation of being observed, that any night... He'd pretty much asked Gabriel not to bring up the subject and the others had been instructed on pretence by Josh; so why would they think to *ask* if they wanted it again? He'd pretty much asked not to be informed.

And the crazy thing was that as much anxiety as not knowing gave him, he wasn't sure he'd have been able to cope with the concrete knowledge about when he'd receive another visit. Not and spend time in Gabriel's living room sharing pizzas after the alphas returned from the site every night, not and play video games with Josh like everything was alright. Sergi had made them stop by Ray's mum's house to pick up a homemade peach pie—Ray's favourite—and between that and the alcohol, it had turned the next night into something akin to a celebration.

Ray was a little tipsy himself—having downed a glass of their homebrew wine didn't do much to his metabolism—but the others were laughing way too much at the movie they'd found on TV and jostling on the couch like they were pre-teens instead of grown men. Josh was snuggled against Ray's side, half dozing on his shoulder, until he was quite awake and nuzzling at the mark he'd left on Ray's neck. He kept at it even as Ray froze in place, but even drunk, Josh was too perceptive to miss his discomfort for long. He raised his head, still close enough to see the specks of gold in his brown eyes even in the low light of the television, and asked quietly, "Let me kiss you."

Ray's breath caught. Of all the places in which he'd expected this to happen... His lips parted, maybe to say no, maybe to ask why Josh was bothering to ask for permission. But then he saw the hurt expression on Josh's face and realised his friend thought he was being rejected. Ray had no choice but to let Josh fuck him, but that wasn't what Josh wanted. Josh wanted Ray to want him back. It was absurd, in the middle of the mess his life had become, to think that not long ago a moment like this would have been a fantasy come true.

It wasn't really their first kiss and it wasn't really the beginning of anything, but Ray leaned in anyway and placed his mouth on Josh's, flickering his tongue to gain entrance. Josh groaned into his mouth, surging up to kiss him back as his hands snatched fistfuls of Ray's clothes and just like that they were making out heatedly enough that Alec, sitting on Ray's other side, got to his feet to move out of their way. Josh was under Ray now, strong and steady, always there for him. His body was hard—not just aroused, but muscled and firm, shaped by hard work into a beautiful machine. Vaguely, Ray knew they were being watched, but he couldn't care right then, not when Josh was slipping his hands under his shirt and then under his waistband, thrusting his hips up to push their hard cocks together through the layers of clothing. He was chafing a little but he didn't really care, he couldn't stop, he needed... He only noticed he was wet between his arse cheeks when a strong pair of hands forced him to get his knees under him so they could sneak down and open his trousers. He moaned at the cold air on his cock and kissed Josh harder still—like he could wish the strange sensation away—as his friend slid his hands down to squeeze Ray's arse. He knew there were other hands pulling his trousers down his legs, then lifting his knees one by one to leave his bottom half completely exposed, but Josh was plenty of distraction. Then Josh was tangling their legs, pressing Ray's naked groin against his clothes in a move as deliciously erotic as it was painful on his sensitive flesh. He rolled them over fast enough they'd have fallen off the couch if not for a well-timed shove from one of their audience. The sound of the zip of Josh's pants made Ray clench helplessly, like his body knew what it needed was close, like... Josh raised his head, his lips were reddened and his eyes wild, but he still met Ray's eyes.

"Can I?" he rasped out, arms trembling as he held himself above Ray. Out of the corner of his eye, Ray caught Gabriel's face. He forced his eyes back to Josh. He didn't know what the question was, except that answer was his body's, it was in the insistent throb of emptiness between his legs. He gave a soft nod. He was scared, of course, he couldn't forget the others were there, but he trusted Josh. Josh yelped when Gabriel stepped behind him this time to lower his trousers and underwear for him.

"What..." he asked, and Gabriel leaned in close enough to whisper something in his ear that made him pause and allow Gabriel to finish undressing him. He sat back on Ray's thighs to get his own shirt off. His chest gleamed and his nipples were hard. He was like something out of a dream, beautiful and perfect and kind. Ray's best friend in the whole world.

Josh leaned in for another kiss, and Ray took hold of his neck to keep him close as his left leg was lifted off the couch and he was opened up for it. Josh was still kissing him when he lined himself up and entered him, easy as coming home, two pieces fitting together perfectly. Ray's muscles unwound with the usual haziness alphas brought out in him, going pliant and easy even as he continued to return Josh's kisses. It was hard to breathe, and harder still to stay still as Josh took him over, going deeper and deeper with each thrust, his tongue echoing the movements in Ray's mouth.

Afterwards, Gabriel gave him some water and then asked for his own kiss and Ray nodded. It wasn't so bad, he thought, as his body opened up like a flower to the second alpha. It was easy, really.

They all asked him, and it didn't hurt, not when he gave in.

Chapter 6

His body was changing fast. Unlike human females, a male omega's pregnancy only lasted six months—something to do with the wolf's biology and the accelerated metabolism of werewolves. Ray didn't know whether he was grateful it wasn't going to last longer or upset that the changes were happening so fast. Women, he imagined, at least got a chance to get used to the idea before they had to feel their bellies stretching from within.

It had only been two months and he'd had to discard most of his jeans, but worse still was the knowledge that the alphas had noticed. Sergi had casually offered to drive him to the shopping centre for clothes when he went himself to get some more materials for the house. Iesu hadn't even been that subtle: when the button on Ray's jeans hadn't survived his attempts to unhook it, he'd commented, "Well, it was under a lot of pressure already."

Ray had almost kicked him in the face. Accidentally, of course. But at least Iesu didn't try and touch him there, which Gabriel had done just the day before, cupping his belly as he fucked Ray on all fours. Ray had let himself drop face-first on the bed, forcing Gabriel to take his hands away or follow suit. Gabriel hadn't made him get back up, just lowered himself and kept fucking him like that. He didn't know if his cousin understood, but he hadn't been able to make himself ask.

It was only when he walked into the kitchen one morning to the scent of cooking bacon—one of the other alphas must have stayed the night because Gabriel wasn't one for cooking—and had to run to the toilet to throw up that it really hit him. He hadn't closed the door so he wasn't surprised when he heard steps hurrying his way; whoever was home couldn't have missed the sounds of retching. "Damn, Ray, are you okay?"

It was Iesu. That probably meant Josh wasn't around, because as a rule it was always Josh who came to him in moments like this.

"It's mostly bile," Ray said. He rolled over and closed the lid before reaching over to flush.

"Was it the bacon?" Iesu asked, either not noticing his tone or ignoring it. "Because it was out of date, it's from Monday. Alec got those five packages that were reduced. But he said it smelled fine and that was more important than a date..."

When Ray stayed on the floor, trying to will his stomach to stop cramping, Iesu came closer and offered a hand. Ray hesitated, then took it and let the alpha help him to his feet. Before, Iesu had been about Ray's own size, but now he looked muscled and powerful next to Ray's rapidly rounding body. Ray shivered at feeling him so close. Iesu must have noticed— how could he not?—he didn't mention it. He got the glass Gabriel had to brush his teeth and rinsed it before offering it to Ray full of cold tap water. Ray drank gratefully, leaning back against the sink and keeping his eyes lowered so he didn't have to look at the other man.

"If none of you can smell it's off, it's probably fine. I just..."

"You're sensitive," Iesu offered. "I remember when my sister was pregnant, she kept banning random foods."

Ray stiffened. None of them had talked about it like that. It wasn't even the reference to Ray's state, it was how *casual* Iesu was being about it. Before they'd only brought it up when it was absolutely necessary. A necessary evil. But this... He put down the glass and turned to leave without replying. He'd just go to his room and wait until the smells died down. He wasn't hungry anyway.

"Ray!" Iesu called. Ray paused. He didn't think Iesu had meant to, but it felt like an order to Ray and that meant he had to obey. "I... crackers helped, I'll get you some."

Ray shrugged. "Okay, thanks," he managed, voice coming out flat and dry. It wasn't really Iesu's fault, not beyond the fact that he'd personally satisfied the urges of Ray's own biology and enjoyed doing it. But you didn't need to be trying to hurt someone to do it—all it took was chance or carelessness, or just plain ignorance.

The crackers did help. If he had them early in the morning, he could mostly trust his stomach to behave the rest of the day unless he encountered a particularly disgusting food. It wasn't even foods he disliked. After the bacon, he'd ended up being sick when his mother had come over and made broccoli—convinced as she was that they were not eating well.

But his body wasn't done with him. His belly grew rounder and harder, and then, one morning he felt them move inside him. He knew that the normal reaction was telling someone about it, but instead he wanted to hide it, to hide himself and everything his stupid body was doing to him.

And he couldn't.

Because since he'd started fucking the alphas wide awake instead of letting them do him while pretending to be asleep, they'd developed a bit of a schedule. It wasn't every single night, they understood that there were five of them and only one of him and that he wanted time to paint and do other things, and that sometimes he just didn't want to be touched.

He knew that if he asked tonight, or simply pulled away from their touch, none of them would force him or even insist. But he knew well what would happen if he postponed giving them what they needed from him: they would grow more and more desperate as time went by and when they were finally allowed to have him—and that time would always come—they would need it too much to control themselves. They wouldn't hurt him, of course, but the sex got rougher if Ray made them do without.

He didn't mind a little shoving and biting, really. What scared him was the way the alphas' need meant their desire would overwhelm his own and he'd grow heavy and passive. He'd lie there like he had during the full moon, feeling what they were doing to him almost as much from their perspective as his own.

He didn't always want it when they started, but he liked kissing and he liked their bodies. Who could dislike their well-shaped shoulders and various shades of golden skin? And if they could manage to go slow, if their own desire could grow with his... Well, it felt natural. Real. And if he was sore or tired, Ray could offer a handjob and it'd be enough for them to be able to come on him and kiss him for a while. Sometimes, when it was soft and tender like that, their orgasm wouldn't even trigger his own.

But if they were desperate for it, their wolves demanding they possess their omega... Ray would end up sprawled on the bed with a cock up his arse and another in his mouth because they were incapable of waiting for a turn. They'd all feel shitty about it afterwards. They didn't want to hurt him—he believed that. And Ray didn't want to make them suffer for something they couldn't help but need from him. They'd given him what he needed when he'd gone into heat. It didn't really matter that Ray hadn't *wanted* it. They enjoyed taking him. He didn't delude himself that they were only doing it because their inner wolf demanded they keep mounting their omega. But high as he was on hormones a lot of the time, he hadn't missed that Josh didn't go to him as often as the others and that when he didn't show up, he also avoided Ray during daytime. It wasn't just Ray fighting it.

Josh was perhaps the one trying the hardest, but that didn't mean he got the best results. He had been the first to demonstrate the effect delayed gratification had on an alpha wolf when it finally got what it wanted. Afterwards, he'd been so mortified that it had taken him two whole days to be able to sit Ray down and apologize for walking in on him in the shower and fucking him right there without really asking. It was a lesson well learned, and now Josh would stretch it out a bit—maybe a couple of days—but never more. Ray didn't mind much: when you had five full-time lovers, it didn't really change much if one of them was missing one fuck a month. But the idea of asking for it tied his stomach into knots. He just couldn't do it.

But that wouldn't matter very soon. All of them were helpless when it came to the moon. There wasn't much of a point in trying to deny the goddess of the sea, and thank the gods Alec had warned them all before it'd happened. When the moon went high, Ray went into heat—it didn't matter if he was pregnant now—and his alphas were along for the ride.

And of course, with two days to the next full moon, if he didn't have sex with some of the alphas tonight, they'd be so desperate for it he was likely to spend the whole week after sleeping it off. Gabriel would stay away, most likely, he didn't like to seem desperate for Ray, and he made a point of being stronger in resisting his wolf than the other alphas—except Josh, who wasn't resisting as much as openly defying. But Josh was due, and with the moon rising and knowing it'd help when it did, the other three didn't have many reasons to resist.

Sergi and Iesu came together. Sergi made a point of glancing at Ray's current project and smiling his pleasure so widely that the other alpha elbowed him, rolling his eyes.

"Show off much?" he teased.

"How am I showing off if it's Ray's painting?" Sergi snipped back.

"Um, because you gave him the supplies?" Iesu replied. "And nobody's been able to top that. Not even Josh."

"Who says they haven't?" Ray interrupted. It was weird to have them speaking about him like he wasn't there.

They both turned to him, Iesu already asking excitedly, "Did you like the clothes? I thought you looked uncomfortable."

And Ray immediately felt terrible. It was pretty much true that Sergi's offering had been the best thing any of the alphas had given him and they both looked so *eager* to please him. He shrugged. "It's not a competition."

Sergi's grin spoke volumes as to his opinion on the matter: it would continue to be a competition as long as he was winning it. Maybe it was an alpha instinct to make everything a comparison. Ray didn't much see the point, and maybe that was a clue he should have paid attention to before. Presenting omega had felt like an accident, an unexpected tragedy; but what if it wasn't because the pack needed a male omega? What if it had been in him all along? It wouldn't change anything, not really. But it filled him with dread anyway, like he might have brought it upon himself, like it wasn't just the luck of the draw but what he deserved, what he was meant *for*.

He shifted on the bed, sitting up straighter and he couldn't imagine what he could have done to provoke it but suddenly he was getting wet for them. It happened fast enough to be uncomfortable. He knew they could both smell it and he felt like he was giving himself away despite the fact that growing slick had very little to do with *Ray's* feelings or desires.

Iesu crawled on the bed from one side, Sergi from the other, and Ray allowed the pillows to be pushed aside so he could lie flat on his back where they wanted him.

He'd stopped pretending it wasn't happening, but he hadn't figured out what to do, what was expected of him, what was okay, or what he *wanted*. It had been so simple before:

getting hard and wanting to get some stimulation on his cock—someone else's touch or his own. Now he had to deal with the fact that he could get aroused because an alpha wanted him, *for an alpha*.

He wished he could just suffer through it—not because he wanted the pain, of course, but he wished he could know what was truly his and what was the new magic of his body twisting his desire to his alphas' will. If he knew the difference, he thought, he might have been able to bear it better. He couldn't really deal with how real it felt, how it felt *his*.

Sergi gently tipped his head back and took his mouth, tongue tracing his teeth. He felt Iesu open the maternity trousers he'd bought for him, then lower his underwear. He'd worn no shoes, knowing this was coming. Sergi helped him roll onto his side and it was easy, almost natural for him to push a knee between Ray's naked thighs and rub his hard cock against the curve of Ray's stomach. He moaned against Ray's throat as Ray struggled to get enough breath. Sergi pulled back and started shifting his hips forward, trailing precome over Ray's exposed chest as he climbed up the bed until his groin was level with Ray's face. Behind him, Iesu was fitting himself closer, hard cock like a brand against Ray's buttocks. He clenched, feeling the wetness coating his insides. Iesu moaned and shoved his cock into the space between Ray's arse cheeks. Just as Sergi thrust forward and the head of his cock brushed Ray's chin.

"Oh, god, *Ray*," Iesu said and Ray heard himself make a sound he couldn't describe in response. And then he couldn't anymore because Sergi was guiding his cock into his mouth, gently but firmly feeding Ray his length, and he had to concentrate not to choke on it. He struggled—lying on his side made it hard to really open his throat up to the invasion. He was concentrating hard enough on breathing through his nose that he missed what Iesu was doing until the head of his dick popped into his hole. He arched, body opening to his alpha's cock as a wave of pleasure overwhelmed him. Sergi groaned at the loss of his mouth before taking hold of his hair and guiding his mouth back to his crotch. Ray slurped more than sucked on it, as Iesu's cock made its way fully inside him. He was trapped under them, their rhythm not quite matching so that when Iesu pulled out, Sergi pushed in, making Ray feel like he was drowning in sensation. He struggled weakly under their bodies, making them whimper as his arse and throat contracted around their cocks.

And then, for no reason he could figure out in his oxygen-deprived state, Sergi pulled out of his mouth, cock hanging hard and heavy in front of Ray's face as he half turned to Iesu.

"Stop," he asked, his normally low voice sounding thready. Iesu's thighs tensed against Ray's sides as he complied. He was fully seated, throbbing deep in Ray's arse and Ray didn't know if he wanted him to pull out or he just wanted him to go back to fucking him. "We need to fuck him together," Sergi was explaining over his head and Iesu definitely approved if the way his hips stuttered was any indication.

Ray didn't know how they were communicating with each other, just that Sergi turned around and caressed his face, then ran a thumb over his lips and asked, "Ready?" before pushing his cock back into Ray's mouth, already slack for him. At the same time Iesu pulled out until only the tip was in Ray's arse and then both of them pushed forward, stuffing him on both ends. Ray's whole body lit up as they groaned, also in unison.

Iesu had slowed down because he had to keep to Sergi's slower penetration—Ray's lungs were superior to humans' but he still needed to be allowed to breathe occasionally—and he seemed both excited and tortured by the necessity. Ray was too dizzied with both lack of air and lust to tell what they were saying, just got the general impression of approval because his wolf craved it much more than air. But then Iesu suddenly realised that while he couldn't vary his speed, nothing was stopping him from going *harder* and as Ray's body trembled with the aftershocks of that decision, Sergi's breath hitched.

"*Iesu*," he bit off, pushing himself a little faster into Ray's mouth that was comfortable. Iesu shoved into Ray again, and Ray—helpless to do otherwise—shuddered as Iesu's pleasure peaked through his own body, and then choked on the mouthful of come flooding his mouth and throat. Sergi pulled his cock away, spurting all over Ray's shoulder and half his face instead.

Ray's cock, untouched and unattended against his belly, started shooting and as he involuntarily clenched around Iesu's dick in him, his alpha's thrusts sped up, harder and rougher than ever before as if to make up for the earlier control. He didn't feel Iesu come, too overwhelmed by the second orgasm so close to the first.

He tilted his head to the side, blinking to try to get his eyes used to the darkened room and found Sergi's dark lashes in front of him. Iesu was pulling out slowly, sticky and a little painful—he'd given Ray quite a pounding—but he knew in a few minutes it'd just be tender. As he moved away from Ray, he allowed him to roll onto his back again and Ray instinctively looked up at him. Iesu was flushed and bright-eyed and when their eyes caught, he gave Ray a brilliant smile.

"That was amazing," he praised. Ray almost wanted to be angry, but his inner wolf was howling for joy. So he closed his eyes instead.

It didn't matter: the wolf could have what it wanted, Ray couldn't. That was just how it went. And Iesu hadn't meant anything by it—it was just common courtesy to compliment a lover on their performance.

As a beta Ray had felt the full moon rise like an extreme version of a sugar rush, a giddiness and excitement slowly overtaking him that instead of giggling tended to send him running as fast as he could manage. When you were a kid, the full moon run with your pack was the best time of the month, a celebration that started on two feet and moved swiftly on to four without any breaks in between.

It was different now. He was excited all right, but he was also aroused, a low-level malaise that made him shift uncomfortably, get up to pace, rearrange the carefully prepared table Josh and Alec had set up for the after-run festivities. And that was just his body, because in his head he couldn't stop replaying some of the scenes of past heats. His face burned at the way he'd gone lax and pliant under their hands, but it wasn't just that, he was actually starting to burn up with heat. As an omega, mating had become his strongest instinct and when the moon rose fully in a few hours, his wolf's priority.

Except now that he *was* mated, it wasn't so much the sex as his alphas'... his alphas. He could feel them moving about the house right then, and, even though Gabriel's flat was small enough that he always could hear them when they were around, it felt different.

Josh caught him on his way back from the kitchen. "You okay?" he asked, and Ray blinked up at him, feeling disorientated.

He licked his lips, trying to retrieve the words from wherever they had gone. "Just..." he waved a hand vaguely.

Josh nodded sympathetically and Ray noticed his pupils were larger than they should have been in the bright afternoon light. He rubbed Ray's arm softly. "Only a few hours more, okay?"

Ray nodded, mostly because even clear-headed he couldn't have explained the mix of dread and desire that went rushing through him at the prospect.

He was running, free and boundless, and the extra weight he'd gained didn't mean much when he rushed down the hills of his territory. *His*, because now he could tell, his pack patrolled these lands for him and their scent permeated everything. They were upwind and he couldn't really smell them now, not when they were letting him run ahead for a bit before they put some effort into catching him, but they all spent too much time here not to have left an imprint.

And they were letting him: in human form, Ray would have had a fair chance of escaping each of them individually. But his wolf was just playing with his mates; it wouldn't try to actually get away even if Ray had been insane enough to try. And it would have been insane—alphas would follow an omega in heat through pretty much everything but death, but an alpha would follow the omega he'd bred through that and more. It was supposed to be reassuring to know your alpha would always get to you, but to Ray it felt claustrophobic.

It was almost a relief to hear them approach. The wolf surged to the surface, overtaking his sour reflections with the sheer joy of the run, with the challenge of making his mates work for it. And work they did, but they weren't just alphas, they were a pack. The moment they decided they had had enough of play, Ray found Sergi and Alec blocking his way forward as the other three circled him from the sides and behind. Ray wondered if he should shift. Now that he wasn't running he felt oddly uncomfortable in a bitch's body—Alec had tried to explain why an omega male started shifting into a female wolf after he was bred, but Ray had asked him to stop.

He didn't want to be a human surrounded by wolves. He'd heard...

One of them nudged his side, then another got closer from behind. Ray found himself leaning forward, exposing his rump even further, tail lifted invitingly. He wanted to move away, but in this form the wolf's wishes came first and the wolf wanted to stay where it was. It was going to make Ray stand there and let them...

And then he heard a solid hit and the heat of the body behind him disappeared. He turned to look and found that Josh had toppled Gabriel to the ground. Gabriel's jaws snapped at Josh—sharp and deadly but only a warning—and Josh rolled away but didn't retreat. The other alphas were just looking on, possibly as stunned as Ray felt. Ray had to remove the incentive for the fight: with a supreme effort of will, he pushed his wolf aside and felt his limbs lengthening, paws becoming fingers, snout retreating into a nose. By the time he was human again, kneeling on the ground, he saw Sergi starting his own transformation from the corner of his eye. But Gabriel and Josh still weren't paying attention to anything but each other. There was blood on Gabriel's lips, although he couldn't see where on Josh's body it was coming from.

He stepped forward, naked and completely unprotected and threw his arms around Gabriel's neck from behind. The animal tensed, soft fur caressing Ray's skin as he twisted to try and get free, but then something seemed to percolate through his fury. Maybe it was Gabriel's human mind, or maybe the wolf's protective instincts, but he stopped struggling in Ray's arms and instead turned his head enough to lick Ray's neck. Ray opened his eyes to meet his dark gaze before he loosened his hold on him and risked a glance at Josh. Josh had actually stepped back, but he was watching them both attentively.

"Shift," Ray rasped out and let go entirely, getting to his feet, exposing his body completely.

For an endless second, Gabriel continued to look at him, and then his body twisted up as he changed. Ray sighed in relief, terror giving way to the dizzying heat that had been getting worse and worse as they night wore on. Alec, also in two feet, caught him when he stumbled and helped him lie down on the ground. There were no blankets this time but the cold ground was a relief against his skin. And then there was Gabriel's human body, hot but an indescribable relief still, pushing him down, pushing into him in one movement that ended with Gabriel bending him in half to reach his mouth—as if burying himself into Ray's arse wasn't enough.

Maybe because of the scuffle, it was Josh he signalled to when he was done, pulling out of Ray and rolling him onto his side in one movement. He lifted Ray's leg himself as Josh pressed himself against his back and entered his slick hole. Ray clenched around him, shuddering as Josh's strong arms surrounded him as he started moving in him. The orgasm Gabriel had brought out of him had been like a cold shower that immediately evaporated on his fevered skin and now he needed to come again even worse than before.

He remembered the end, and he remembered thinking as his chin was tilted for Alec's cock—he needed some relief—that he recognized Sergi's pace in the way he was being fucked now. After he swallowed, he was given a little water from a bottle, almost as good as coming felt, and then he was being nudged on hands and knees for Iesu and Gabriel was kneeling in front of him and rubbing his cheek as he encouraged him to lean forward to take his cock past his swollen lips.

It hadn't ended there. The full moon was long, and an omega had heats meant for however many alphas had mated him. Ray knew that, but the details were vague. They'd taken what they needed; they'd taken care of him.

He woke briefly when they carried him inside, and for the water and a little bread afterwards, and then he slept.

Chapter 7

E ven with all the precautions, he still woke up sore and tired and could just about manage a little water before he was out again.

The second time he managed to stay awake long enough for Alec to check his pupils and feed him some soft food besides. He looked worried, but Ray was fine, just tired.

The next time he woke up, he was just desperate for the bathroom. He didn't know how long it'd been, but he was sweaty and gross and if they'd tried to get the grass off him, they hadn't done a very good job. Plus, his mouth was dry as a desert. He stumbled to the bathroom and drank from the tap, trembling with relief.

"You're going to make yourself throw up," Someone warned from behind, and Ray summarily ignored it even as his brain told him it was Josh. When he finally looked up, his friend's eyes widened, travelling down his body as if of their volition before Josh quickly looked away. "You... are better."

"How long?"

"Four days," Josh replied, sounding abashed. That was the longest recovery to date. Ray vaguely wondered if they'd messed up the schedule before heat.

"I need a shower," he told Josh and turned around and opened the glass cubicle.

Josh didn't object.

The alphas were mostly busy with the new house, and Ray stayed at Gabriel's, reluctant to let anybody see him in his current state.

But for Anna's birthday, his mother called him and practically begged him to come to dinner. Just the family, she promised, just her and his siblings who all missed him desperately. Anna didn't even remember their father—she'd been too little when he'd died. Ray knew the age difference between them meant that if Anna had anybody she saw as one, it was him. Ray did remember him, though, and he remembered what it'd been like when he'd suddenly been gone, from one day to the next. Ray wasn't dead, of course, but still... he should have visited sooner.

The house was close enough to walk, but he didn't think he could handle the streets, not just yet. To see Josh's expression when he'd asked to be driven over to his mother's house, it seemed the outing was as much a reward to his friend as to his family. Iesu had been equally delighted to take him shopping for a present. Ray felt a little like a child being encouraged for doing well in school, but he pushed those thoughts away and concentrated on thanking them for their efforts.

"You'll save me some pie, right? I know it won't make it to tomorrow with those little monsters you have at home," Josh commented, shooting Ray a happy smile from the driver's seat and it could have almost been any other day since Josh had got his car a few years back—if not for the heavy weight on Ray's middle.

"Sure," Ray said, the quickest way to end the conversation. It was only when that left the silence between them hanging heavily that he realised he'd missed his cue to tease Josh back. He shifted, uncomfortable. Like always now, he needed to pee and the seat belt felt weirdly oppressive across his chest, too. It wasn't only his growing belly, his skin everywhere was sensitive and his nipples in particular were killing him, hardening and softening for no good reason he could see.

If he'd felt the need to touch him before, Josh would have offered a fist bump or a noogie, maybe a pat on the shoulder. Now it was different. Ray was no longer Josh's friend, and there was no reason Josh had to hold back on the impulse to put his hand on the nape of his neck and caress the soft skin there tenderly as he whispered in Ray's ear words that could have time travelled from their own past, "Cheer up, at least you got cake."

The cake was good, but that was about all that could be said about Anna's party.

No, that wasn't really true. He'd missed them all dreadfully, especially Anna, who'd run into his arms the moment he'd stepped through the door. Ray'd picked her up easily despite his belly, holding her legs to the side instead of letting her wrap them around his middle.

A moment later their mother was scolding her for being careless. Ray waved her concern away. "I'm fine. She's tiny, mum."

But of course his sister had looked down, gasping a little at what she saw, and then she'd squirmed until he let her get down on her own feet. She looked up at him guiltily. Ray made himself swallow. He was an adult and there was no room for his weakness and fear here. "I'm fine, Annie, promise. You know how mum gets," he added with an eye roll.

But she hadn't responded in kind, smiling hesitantly as she glanced at the round belly only a little lower than her own head. "Is the baby a boy?"

"Ah, I don't know," Ray admitted. He hadn't even allowed himself to think about it, about what would happen when the pregnancy was over. Anna frowned at him.

"You can't talk to it?"

That had made TJ snort loud enough for Ray to notice his presence. He had tensed, helplessly. TJ was only two years younger than Ray and they'd spent their lives teasing the ever-living-hell out of each other. If he said anything... But TJ was looking more uncertain than Ray had ever seen him, still smelling of beta and freedom, and it wasn't anything he said, it was just that he was *there*. He was home and free to do what he wanted and nobody... Ray shoved the thought away like it burned, it was beneath him. It was pathetic. He loved his brother, he didn't want this for him. For any of them. TJ was already explaining to Anna that people couldn't talk to babies until they came out and that even then the babies didn't really understand.

"But pups do," Anna objected. To Ray's relief, Marisa came over to tell them the cake was ready and Anna needed to make her wishes so they could eat it.

Marisa was TJ's twin, but Ray and she had never been close except in the way they had naturally taken leadership over the younger kids. TJ could be counted on to keep Anna, Harry and Glen from jumping out a window, but nothing as practical as putting them to bed on time; so it had always been up to Ray, as the oldest, and Marisa, as the most sensible. No, not just that, Ray could admit it now if not earlier. It had been Marisa and not TJ because Marisa was a girl and that meant... Well, she hadn't presented yet, but now that Ray was looking back at his own past, he could see the signs: how he'd teased TJ but had taken care of him too, had made sure all the kids had lunches and scarves in winter, and hadn't cared much about whether it was natural for Harry to get into so many fights with other pups. He didn't like to see Harry hurt so if Harry fought, he got grounded.

It'd made sense at the time and his mother had supported him, and now he wondered if TJ's attitude wasn't more... alpha. After him, they could be almost a hundred percent sure all his brothers would present alpha if they presented at all—beta males weren't that rare, either, especially compared to omegas.

"Ray?" Glen asked him, bringing him back to the present. He blinked at his little brother, holding back a flinch when he saw him looking down at his middle. "Does it hurt?" he asked, sounding like he'd asked before.

Ray's throat closed up, mind rushing with contradictory answers. The pregnancy didn't hurt, although it was very uncomfortable, but it'd hurt when... He swallowed, not sure if he wanted saliva or air. The next thing he knew his mother was leaning close, putting her hand on his cheek and saying his name. He could see her lips moving, but her voice didn't quite seem to make it to his ears.

She made him drink some tea and then, once sound had returned and his heart had stopped trying to stab him, walked him over to his old room to rest in the dark. He didn't think he would be able to sleep, not in a place that was like a sore in itself. But he must have because the next thing he knew was that Josh was gently shaking him awake. "Come on, mate, time to go home."

He didn't see any of his siblings on the way out, and he didn't think it was because it was late. His mother was quiet for once, no reassurances, not even her usual expressions of unconditional love as she walked them to the door. He felt her gaze on him as Josh led him to the car, but he didn't look back.

He couldn't. He felt if he tried, he'd freeze, trapped forever between what he'd been and what he was, forever longing for something that no longer existed.

Ray answered her calls when she called, but they didn't mention a visit again. Sometimes Josh showed up with her food, smelling of her hands and her love, and Ray would thank her on the phone for it. But he didn't touch it, insisting the alphas have it instead. Ray knew they all thought it was odd, not just Josh—who knew his mother was sending over all his favourites—but they had the courtesy not to bring it up.

Ray didn't think it was too much to ask. He was still doing his part, after all.

Chapter 8

Alec said the pregnancy was going well, and the growth was normal, and then in what seemed like the course of a week, Ray's belly grew large enough that he woke one morning and had to catch himself on his nightstand to keep his balance, arching his back to compensate. He didn't like to think about the time when he'd realised he was too big to see his cock anymore. At least he could still reach it to piss—lucky too since he needed to all the time. The babies kicked inside him, probably displeased that he'd jostled them, and Ray almost whimpered at the effect that had on his bladder. He straightened, not bothering with shoes—even sleepers were a pain when you couldn't see where you were stepping—and aimed for the toilet.

He'd been in sweats for weeks—wedged under his belly—and wearing Gabriel's T-shirts for a little less than that, so tight and badly fitting clothes hardly registered anymore. He just wanted to get downstairs in one piece and get enough breakfast for six. It was getting easier to think like that, maybe because it was pretty hard to ignore someone when they were kicking you from inside your own body, maybe one *could* get used to anything given enough time.

He was glad to see Alec was in the kitchen—of all the alphas, he made the best breakfast—or he was until Alec turned around and his eyes widened big as plates. He didn't know why he'd even bothered to ask for Ray's preference; Alec didn't do subtle.

"What?" Ray snapped, impatient and uncaffeinated and just *done*. Wasn't Alec an expert on the body?

"Sorry, just, it... popped out," Alec explained, gesturing down at Ray's belly while visibly making an effort to keep his eyes on Ray's face.

Ray didn't bother to look down. "And?"

"Um, well, it's..." Alec licked his lips, nervous and, Ray thought bitterly, *excited*. "It happens before it's time."

Ray grasped for a chair to fall into, not needing to ask time for what. Of course it would be time soon, what had he been thinking? That he'd stay like this forever? Despite how strong he was, he wasn't sure he would be able to move around much longer with his awkward appendage. Alec had learned something in the last few months, at least, because after that he filled Ray's plate in silence, giving him coffee and not tea without asking first.

It was only a little over two kilometres across the river to the site where they'd christened the land and where the house now was, but Ray was heavy enough now that Gabriel insisted on driving him over. They had to take a detour through the centre of town and Gabriel spent the ride telling him what they still had left to do. Ray kept his gaze outside and his hand on his belly. The movement of the car was jostling the babies and his insides along with them and he wasn't used to it anymore. He thought he hadn't been in a car since Anna's birthday, two... no, three months ago.

He was so absorbed in the outside that he didn't realise they'd arrived until Iesu jumped to open his door for him. Only a glare dissuaded him from trying to unhook the seatbelt for Ray, too, but Ray had to accept the hand he offered to dismount the stupid Jeep. He was tall enough to reach the floor, of course, but now that he could no longer see the ground where he stepped and that his balance was compromised—the babies were growing too fast for Ray to ever get used to his centre of gravity—he couldn't risk new terrain without extra support.

Iesu let go of him as soon as Ray stepped away from the car, but stayed close, pretending not to hover. And then Ray stopped short at the sight of the building. It was all on the ground level, but it was way larger than he'd expected. All red brick and black tiles, the door a deep dark brown—oak, maybe, but painted. They must have heard the car because Josh was there then and Ray allowed him to take hold of his arm to guide him inside.

"I think you'd like this room, it's big enough for a partition..." Gabriel had guided them both to a room large enough to be the living area, except they'd been in the living room already.

The windows in this room were insane, too—he could just imagine how the light would hit. And it being a corner room meant that he'd get some quiet, too. "I don't think I need a partition," he said, letting go of Josh's arm to go look out the window. "I can just set up here."

"Oh, sure," Gabriel agreed. "I just thought you'd want to have the children's room decorated."

And Ray's stomach fell so abruptly he had to take hold of the windowsill to stay on his feet. He heard Josh's alarmed exhaled a second before his friend's hands were on his hips. "What's wrong?"

"The children again, of course," he murmured, "For one second I thought he was talking about me."

"Come on, Ray" Gabriel insisted. "Of course you can have a studio, and whatever you like. But I thought you'd want them close."

"Close?" Ray asked, turning around and clumsily dislodging Josh—only managing because Josh hurried to step back. "I don't want them at all!"

"You will," Gabriel doggedly insisted, "when you see them, you'll want them more than anything."

"So you are saying my hormones are going to, what, mind fuck me into wanting something I don't?"

"Instincts aren't lies," Gabriel said calmly. "Just because you're in denial about what you actually are—"

"Gabriel," Josh interrupted, stepping between them. "Is something burning in the kitchen?"

Gabriel blinked but he let Josh get away with the interruption and the implied order. "Of course," he said with a nod at Ray.

Once they were alone, Ray turned to his friend. "I don't need babysitting."

Josh shrugged. "He was being a dick."

Ray hesitated. He could hardly deny it or say it wasn't Josh's job to tell people off when they were awful to Ray. Independently of the fact that Josh was his alpha now, it was exactly the way Josh had always behaved. He'd always had Ray's back. Just like Ray had his.

He swallowed and turned back to the window. It was all green outside, flat until the trees started growing closer together. It was beautiful, not so far from the land he'd grown up in. Not so far from home... But not home. He wondered if it'd feel more like his own territory soon, if his wolf would make being an omega okay. If it would make this land a home.

Josh was too wise to speak to Ray when he was this close to snapping, so he just let Ray look out the window and breathe as deeply as he could and think about not being so heavy anymore, about it being over.

Each room had to be christened with Ray's seed before they could put down the tiling, so his essence would be as close to the foundation as possible. But Alec had determined Ray was too big to be fucked. Not that Ray had needed a medical opinion. The last time had been extremely uncomfortable—even with the alpha's hands fully supporting his belly as he stood on all fours for it.

Instead he'd take them into his mouth and swallow. In a way, oral sex was harder, it was definitely more work since his mouth hadn't suddenly changed to accommodate cocks the way his arse had. He'd thought he'd get to stay clothed, at least, which was a relief because he couldn't look at himself in the mirror anymore.

Sergi sounded almost apologetic as he disabused him of this notion, "We can't waste your come and if you're dressed it'll get on your clothes for sure."

Ray opened his mouth to object, then he sighed, defeated already. It wasn't worth arguing.

"You can keep your shirt on," Sergi offered. Ray shrugged and Sergi helped him stand from the armchair in the corner and started lowering his trousers, still talking. "After this, you'll be able to tell who is in which room of the house," he explained.

Ray felt his sweats being pushed down his hips, then Sergi's hands came back up to send his boxers on the way too and he was standing on a pool of clothes. "I'm going to call in Iesu to keep an eye on you, okay?"

Ray didn't object; Sergi and Iesu had been sharing him for months now. They seemed to have found a good balance between their preferences for Ray's arse and mouth. He was glad they'd not be put to a test now that Ray's arse wasn't available.

When Iesu came in, they helped Ray sit with his back to the wall and Sergi kneeled over him and kissed him softly on the lips, sweeping his tongue in as if in question. Ray didn't respond to the kiss and Sergi retreated, jumping to his feet.

"Well, let's do this," he said and lowered his zip and brought out his cock. He was hard as flint, just like Ray expected after his condition had made them reduce the number of times each alpha got to have him.

Ray wanted to look away—mostly because he didn't want to think about what he looked like, belly sticking out under the thin cotton shirt and the floor growing slick under his arse—but sucking cock, or even getting his face fucked, wasn't an activity that allowed him to go away in his own head. If he didn't pay attention, he'd choke. Then Sergi would stop and apologize, offer to get him water, make a fuss, and everything would take that much longer.

Sergi put a chair in front of Ray's face, high enough that Ray only had to strain a little forward to take the tip of his dick into his mouth. After that, it was almost easy, Sergi pushing closer and Ray holding on to the chair not to strain his neck. Sergi warned him before coming—Ray always swallowed for them, of course, but today it was particularly important that he got it all so that his pack was mixed inside his body when he himself orgasmed. It was still a bit of a struggle when Sergi pushed his left hand under Ray's chin and forced his lips shut as he spilled even as Ray's own orgasm rippled through him. Ray was trembling, the shirt he'd been allowed to keep a sweaty mess, but he managed to raise his hand to tap Sergi's thigh to let him know he'd swallowed. Sergi's grip loosened and Ray heard the chair scrape against the bare boards as he retreated. A moment later he felt hands on his own thighs collecting his seed. It was Iesu and once he had a handful he went to the corners of the room and used it to paint the floor.

Ray closed his eyes again and didn't move until they put water to his lips. Sweet and cold relief, even better when he coughed a little and it spilled down his neck. Sergi cursed softly, then said, "Let me take your shirt off, it's a mess now."

And Ray sighed and let him help him out of it, still shaky and tired and knowing it couldn't be over yet because they needed to get the other rooms, too.

In the next room, Iesu kissed him softly, holding his naked hips gently, thumbs rubbing against the distended skin of Ray's belly. Long and wet and thorough like he wanted to get to every trace of Sergi's come left in Ray's mouth. Sergi had followed them here and was watching them avidly from a few steps away until Iesu pulled back with a last peck to Ray's lips and turned to him.

"I want you to blow him while I hold him," he asked and Ray heard Sergi gasp.

Iesu left his front and stood against the wall, then led Ray to step back into his body, being a little shorter than Ray, his hard cock pressed right against Ray's naked buttocks through his jeans. And then Sergi was falling to his knees in front of him and Ray's arousal was peaking, wetting his entrance and hardening his cock in Sergi's firm grip. He whined low in his throat, suddenly needing to be touched beyond Sergi's hands and Iesu's mostly clothed body behind him.

"Shhh..." Iesu reassured him, arm sneaking around Ray's chest. "I got you, sweetie."

Ray felt him fumbling with his zip and the heat of the bare skin of his erection was an almost indescribable relief. He knew Alec had said no fucking, but in that moment, with an alpha ready to put it in him... it didn't matter. But Iesu aimed his cock down, lodging it between Ray's slick arse cheeks instead of putting it inside him. The sensation set half the nerves in Ray's body on fire, including the ones inside him that just *ached* for contact.

As if he knew what had just happened—Ray and Iesu might have made enough noise to alert him—Sergi chose that moment to take the tip of Ray's cock into his mouth and suck. Ray pushed forward and Iesu's hand tightened on his hip and chest as he groaned his approval. "Yeah, *more*. Sergi... give him more."

And Sergi did. It was not Ray's first blowjob, but Sergi was sucking like it might be his last and even though he wasn't anywhere close to Ray's prostate, his arsehole felt like it suddenly contained a million more nerve endings than it ever had before. Every one of Iesu's thrusts shocked him with a new wave of pleasure. They found a rhythm easily, as if they'd been practicing, and Ray found himself trapped between Sergi's mouth and Iesu's cock, the wetness on both ends, his and theirs. Iesu was leading, speeding up and forcing both Ray and Sergi to follow, until he suddenly froze, groaning an order like it almost hurt him to say, "Stop!"

Ray froze, unable to ignore the direct order. A moment later Sergi was pulling back from his cock and Iesu was laughing in his ear. "Not you, Ray, you can keep going, love. We just can't let Sergi swallow what we need."

And with that, one of his hands let go of Ray's chest and cupped the flesh of his arse instead, pressing it in to give his cock a tighter place to fuck, then started shoving his cock through the mess between Ray's cheeks in earnest, harder and faster than he'd managed even with Sergi holding Ray in place for him. It only took a few thrusts and then Iesu was coming, and so was Ray, of course, swept up into his pleasure his body erupted, giving the alphas what they needed of him.

It was too much. He swayed and Iesu's hands surrounded his belly, trying to keep him upright, but in the end it took Sergi surging up from where he'd moved a little to the side to hold him up. "Fuck," he mumbled against Ray's belly. "Sorry, I... sorry..."

They helped him sit down and gave him some more water, holding him between their bodies as he trembled, adrenaline and fear and simply the cold because he was completely naked in a half-finished house, even with Iesu curled up against his back and Sergi against his front, hands cupping his belly as effectually as a child's coat might have covered an adult. "That was good," Iesu mumbled, "you were really good, Ray," he insisted, kissing Ray's neck and cheek and Ray let him, so exhausted he didn't think he'd be able to get off the floor even with their help. He felt Sergi getting up and walking around but he kept his eyes closed as he was cradled in his alpha's arms. He'd done his duty and now he could rest.

After they took him home, Ray slept through dinner that night. The pregnancy was advanced enough that he couldn't take any excitement without it leaving him knackered, but the next morning Josh brought him breakfast in bed and explained that Alec had banned *any* sexual activity until Ray delivered the babies after Iesu and Sergi had recounted the events of the previous afternoon.

In a way, it was a relief; but there was also the "after" which Ray could barely think about because of the babies.

I t wasn't until Josh and Gabriel came over with an IKEA catalogue open on Josh's old laptop that Ray realised how urgent the move was.

"Sorry," Josh said immediately catching Ray's confusion. "It'd really help if the babies were born there. Like, really make it our territory."

Ray had heard of the magical power of birth, of course, but then... "Then what was that about yesterday?"

"We needed a couple rooms, at least," Gabriel explained in his practical tone. "It doesn't matter so much for rooms where we will be spending only some time, but bedrooms are where we will be most vulnerable."

"Are you telling me that every First Omega has to do this?" Ray asked sceptical.

Gabriel sighed. "Not quite, but I talked it over with my dad, and I asked for the best. I want to make sure you are safe," he said, so simply Ray couldn't think of how to object.

"So now we will have to wait until I can do it again to finish the other rooms?"

"No," Gabriel admitted, finally looking a little regretful. "Turns out he didn't really mean come when he said bodily fluid, he meant blood."

"Are you fucking kidding me?" Ray snapped, pushing his chair back and stumbling to his feet. Josh instinctively extended his hand and just as instinctively pulled it back at Ray's glare. "You mean I did all that for *nothing*?"

"Not for nothing," Gabriel said calmly. "It worked. It's just that it could have been blood."

"I can't *believe* you. Do you have any fucking idea how *not* in the mood I am right now?" Ray demanded, feeling himself go red.

"Yes, actually," Gabriel said softly, refusing to fight, "which is why I haven't paid you a visit in two weeks."

Ray stopped, frowning. He hadn't been keeping track, but it had been a while since Gabriel had come to him. "Why not?" he asked quietly.

"We are *trying*, Ray," Josh said from where he was still sitting.

Ray exhaled, wincing as he got kicked. The babies didn't like the yelling, he'd learned it early, and they didn't care that Ray was uncomfortable and upset, too hot and too cold by turns. That he hadn't wanted to have sex for weeks, but had known he couldn't say no when he wouldn't be able to do it soon. But Ray cared, and not just because he'd rather avoid them kicking him for it, but because he wanted to protect them. And if it meant biting his tongue about this, letting it go, letting his alphas' efforts be enough...

He sat back down, eyes on the window of Gabriel's tiny house. "Get Alec in here," he said, rolling up his sleeve.

Chapter 9

Ray told Josh to get leather and other furniture that could be easily washed, or otherwise get covers. He knew way too well how little anything lasted around children and he'd never had to deal with a whole litter before. Other than that, he didn't care. The rooms all had floors, the bathroom and kitchen had running water, and the electric generator was working, even if it needed a human from town to come over and adjust it after Iesu's dad sloppy work.

He had other things to worry about: namely, eating and sleeping, which was all he was in the mood to do after they finally moved to the new house.

He shifted into the wolf in his sleep, and when he woke in fur it wasn't just his species that had changed. It wasn't the first time, but he felt the absence between his legs as keenly as the weight in his middle. The bitch whimpered, confused and upset, the scents suddenly too strong after months of not shifting except in the full moon and, before Ray could get hold of himself, there were several alphas in the room. Alec exuded concerned, as usual. Iesu and Josh were just alert. Ray snapped at Alec's reaching hand, but allowed Josh to bury his fingers in the scruff of his neck. He didn't even notice when Iesu sat next to Josh and leaned against him to start rubbing his side.

"Can I touch you now?" Alec asked, teeth gritted. He wasn't a bad guy, but his fear unnerved the wolf as much as his excessive concern unnerved Ray as a human. He gave the alpha a long look, then laid his head on his paws. Alec's hands were quick and efficient, nothing like the leisurely petting his other alphas were providing.

But it was Alec who said, "I don't think it'll happen today. But in the next couple of days... I'll check on you later."

Ray didn't acknowledge the information; it was okay as a wolf, or at least not expected, and he was glad to have the excuse not to speak. Alec got to his feet and Ray shoved his ears more firmly under Josh's hands, forcing himself to focus on that, on the sensations, not to think. *Wolves don't think*, he reminded himself, and groaned when Iesu's hands found a good spot in his middle, rolling over to give him access and startling a laugh out of the alpha.

"You are such a puppy," Josh told him fondly, and Ray clicked his teeth at him menacingly. "Yeah, yeah, I know you bite, don't worry. You're a terrifying puppy."

Ray would have liked to take offence but he felt too good to manage anything stronger than irritation. He closed his eyes and rested, for once the wolf and he were in agreement that the days ahead would be hard.

It was different when it was time. He'd found a spot he liked for it already, but other than what his instincts told him, he had no fucking idea what he was doing. The wolf might have been fine with that, but Ray was terrified. And then Alec was there, begging Ray to let him in and squeezing through into the small den even though Ray could have torn him to pieces. Except the wolf wouldn't have, not really; Alec was his mate.

And he was a good mate, Ray had to admit, he guided Ray into an easier position and encouraged him with firm words and then he disentangled the pups and put them close enough they could latch onto Ray's swollen tits. After it was over, he took a water bottle off his backpack and made Ray drink from it. And that was all Ray could manage before he fell asleep despite the odd sensation of being sucked on.

In the morning he let Alec—who'd spent the night curled up in a corner to be on hand if he was needed—help him get the pups out of the den. The others were waiting outside and when, despite their tiny size, they each picked up one of the babies, Ray understood they could tell which one they had fathered. Alec had explained once the babies were being held, Ray could switch back. But he didn't; he felt vulnerable enough as it was without having to walk naked across their yard to get to the house. He changed back only once he was in the bathroom. Despite being on his knees, he had to close his eyes at the shift in his balance. His belly was still a little swollen, but barely noticeable at all, and that meant he suddenly had no need to pull his back so straight to keep from overbalancing.

Nobody interrupted his shower, and if he didn't linger it was simply because there were five creatures out there who'd spent their whole existence inside his body and who were not connected to him anymore but still belonged to him. He could hear their heartbeats even through the sound of the shower, and he could have sworn he'd feel it if they needed him, but he wasn't *sure*.

The babies were already dressed up, all curled up in the cot they'd set up in the common area so any of them could access it during the night. It was the first time Ray got to see their faces—they'd changed into humans the moment he had—and he found himself taking hold of the cot to keep his balance.

They were still so small, even though they'd felt enormous inside. And then they realised he was there—recognizing his scent even though he'd showered—and they started to cry. They were hungry, he could tell.

He'd frozen, watching the alphas scamper to pick them all up and try and soothe them with no success until Gabriel spoke up, "Stop shushing them, they aren't making a fuss. They need to feed."

"I thought..." Ray started, voice too small, suddenly feeling the weight of the milk in his chest. He hadn't even touched himself to wash properly and he'd bundled himself up in a hoodie to hide how the area around his nipples, normally tight with muscle, was swollen and sensitive. He swallowed down the panic, he couldn't afford it now. "It hasn't been two hours."

Alec, who looked profoundly distressed that he couldn't calm down the baby he held, explained almost absentmindedly, "They are not on the clock, and you went away from them for the first time. They probably miss you just as much as..." He glanced up, suddenly shy. "Let's go to the bedroom," he decided and Ray found himself following surrounded, for the first time, by his whole pack.

The king sized bed he'd last seen there was gone, he noticed immediately, instead a wooden structure, much larger, was taking up half the room. And only the bottom was left open because each side was fitted with a baby rail. He stopped, still unused to his own lightness and Sergi caught his arm with his free hand. "You can lower the rails if you want," he explained, and Ray turned his way, towards the now whimpering baby in Sergi's arms and, without exchanging a word, his alpha pressed his chest to Ray's and curled Ray's arm around the tiny creature. The baby sniffled a little more before turning his head towards Ray's covered chest, Ray and Sergi followed his movements, amazed and terrified and watched as a wet stain spread over Ray's hoodie as the pup sucked milk through the worn-out cloth. Sergi breathed out sharply, arms tightening around them and Ray realised what he was seeing and abruptly stepped back, holding the baby carefully against his chest and turning away from Sergi's penetrating gaze.

"You can go," he said, too low for the others to hear over the whimpering and crying, but they must have understood somehow because when Ray climbed onto the bed, they gently deposited the babies by his side, far from the still-open bottom of the bed.

Only Alec stayed behind, awkwardly holding his own bundle. "Where...?"

"Fuck, Alec, just get a pillow," Ray snapped, hunched over uncomfortably over his own chest where Sergi's baby still suckled. He needed to take the hoodie off but he needed to put the baby down first and get Alec out of there first.

"You should..." Alec started and Ray growled at him.

He left.

Ray took off his shirt and reclined back into the positively obscene mountain of pillows. It wasn't easy to manage, but Alec had been right: they wanted to be close to him more than they wanted to suckle and as long as Ray didn't have to watch them do it, the sensation wasn't bad, strange and messy, but not painful or... He held a baby to his chest as he used his free hand to caress its siblings' soft little faces and hands, and then after a while he switched them up, always careful to place them close enough to touch.

And then, when he realised he was too tired to stay awake, he shifted and watched them do it in turn, legs wobbly but necks straight, weak still but protected from something as stupid as falling off a bed.

The alphas had insisted Ray would not have to wake up at all, but of course the babies needed to be fed off Ray's body. Gabriel had tried to tell him that if he went to bed shirtless it would be a matter of whichever baby was hungry being placed in the right position while Ray slept on, and Ray had just about managed not to laugh or snap at him. He woke when Josh brought two of the pups, whimpering loudly, and held out his arms for the first. It latched onto his chest hard enough to make him wince for all that it didn't have teeth. Josh arranged the second one on the other side—by the second day, Ray had been too sleep-deprived to care whether the alphas saw him shirtless anymore—and only then did Ray realise that he did not know their names. He wondered if he'd be able to guess who their fathers that way: there was little in their looks at this stage to tell them apart.

"Who are these guys?" he asked, keeping his eyes on the babies. He'd become more comfortable with the alphas, and he was mostly too tired to care, but sometimes he still couldn't quite deal with the fact that his best friend had fucked and bred him. "You guys were arguing about good names for months, I hope you aren't gonna traumatize them."

"This is James... Jamie," Josh explained, pointing at the baby still suckling desperately. He didn't look any smaller than his brother, but he was definitely hungrier. "And... well, I haven't chosen, really, I've got some ideas but I wanted to ask you first."

Ray's eyes got stuck on the second baby, Josh's baby. And his. And then he made himself look up at Josh. "I can't do that," he told him, "I can't... I can't show preference."

"It's just a name... to, you know, avoid trauma?" Josh said, still hopeful. Still... Ray wasn't blind, and he wasn't stupid: Josh hadn't started feeling this way when he'd become Ray's alpha.

"Have you narrowed it down?"

"Yeah." Josh smiled brilliantly, assuming he'd won. It made sense—Ray had always let him get away with murder, why not such a simply whim? "I've got two that are just about perfect."

But Ray was very serious about this. "Use them both. A middle name. Then if one of them is traumatic, he can use the other one."

Josh's face fell, but he swallowed and pressed on. "Okay. Michael then," he decided, and Ray couldn't keep his eyes from widening at the name of his favourite singer. "And Trevor, after your dad."

And that was just too much, Ray looked down, not at the babies, just away. He wished they'd finish, he just... he needed to be alone for a moment. And Josh could tell, because Josh hadn't just been looking after Ray, he'd been *paying attention*. So he mumbled that he'd be in the common room and to give him a shout when he wanted the babies picked up.

Ray was physically back to normal by the end of the week, but he still wasn't sleeping well. Alec had apologetically explained that breastfeeding could make a huge different to a pup's health and Ray wasn't going to short-charge them, whatever he felt about parenthood; they hadn't asked to be born either and didn't deserve anything but the best. Life was going to be hard enough as it was for some of them: the girls were very likely to be omegas themselves when they grew up, for one thing. They would at least get to choose a mate—Ray would make sure of that—but it was still no joke.

Even so, he was definitely okay enough to bed and he knew it. Iesu and Sergi were probably doing okay but he'd last done anything with the others almost a month back. No penetration, but Gabriel had sucked him off and then he had used the slick Ray's body still produced to jerk himself off all over Ray's swollen belly. Ray hadn't even understood Gabriel was trying to be kind back then. But he'd known about Josh, who always was, and who he thought hadn't touched him sexually for a whole month now.

The babies inside him had made it worse, according to Alec, but Ray didn't know how much better it was for them to have their omega unmarked now that Ray wasn't full of the very proof of their ownership. He didn't know how long he had.

He enjoyed the sex, and if he'd thought it'd end at that, he'd have been able to give himself over into that enjoyment. But it wouldn't. It couldn't. Male omegas went into heat every full moon after they presented, and heat meant breeding. By this time the coming year, he could be delivering his third litter of pups for his alphas. He couldn't even imagine being pregnant again so soon. He was barely getting used to walking around on his own two legs again, and to give that up...

He thought about going back to his mother's pack to ask the only male omega there for advice, but he'd never talked to Paul outside of some platitudes at pack meetings. Ray'd played with his kids, of which there were enough that he wasn't even sure he knew the ones who weren't around his own age. And anyway, Paul only had two alphas—in the middle of the last war there hadn't been enough young men to go around and every omega needed at least one—so however he dealt with it, wouldn't necessarily work for Ray.

So he didn't go, and he didn't say anything. Not even to his mother when she came to their house to meet her grandchildren. Jamie's efforts had paid off and he was the biggest of the lot, but all of them were growing fast. Clara's dark eyes already followed adults around the room. Michael was possibly the sweetest, both as a pup and as a boy. He'd snuggle Maria like she was a cuddly toy, and she showed her affection by licking him as a girl and chewing on his ears as a pup. Sasha had developed a firm preference for being held by Iesu—much to Sergi's displeasure. Funnily enough, Sergi's preference was just as marked now that Ray didn't feel too rotten to notice.

And then Gabriel put a friendly arm around his shoulders to lean in and look at Maria, and he flinched so hard the baby started to cry. He covered up by getting to his feet and walking around until she calmed down, and then it was time to feed them again and that kept him busy for a while. But they eventually fell asleep and he didn't make it to his room before Gabriel approached.

"Ray," his cousin said. He couldn't stop thinking of him that way, even though they were only second cousins and Gabriel was his alpha now. He'd learned to like fucking him, but it was weird when he remembered Gabriel teaching him maths when he'd been a kid. He made himself meet his eyes, feeling almost defiant. He had every reason to be worried, after all, and Gabriel better not try to bullshit him about it. "You look tired. I'm sorry we can't manage without you. Alec says a month should be enough, though."

Ray shrugged. "It's what they need."

Gabriel nodded, staring fixedly back. "What do *you* need?"

Ray couldn't hold his gaze. "What do you mean?"

"Are you worried about something?" Gabriel insisted. "You just... you jumped when I tried to hug you."

"Look, I'm tired and..."

And in a moment Gabriel had stepped close enough to cage him in against the corridor wall... and was holding onto his hand. "Please don't shut me out," he asked so softly Ray had to look at him. It almost didn't sound like his voice.

"I..." he swallowed, and Gabriel's hand caressed his own, his face close but not close enough to kiss. "I don't know what to do."

"About what?"

"I..." Ray closed his eyes, let his head rest on the wall behind him and blurted it out, "Another litter will be a lot."

"Another litter?" Gabriel echoed, sounding confused.

"The full moon is in ten days," Ray said.

"Yes, of course, but... Oh, you think you'll go into heat?"

"Well, yes, it's the *full moon.*"

"Ray." Gabriel's other hand came up and his fingers pushed Ray's hair behind his ear, gentle and soft. "It won't happen so soon after you've given birth."

The words made Ray shift uncomfortably, then they clicked and he met Gabriel's eyes. "What?"

"Your body wouldn't do that to you," Gabriel insisted. "It wouldn't be safe for the babies if you did. They need you."

Ray stared at him, incredulous and almost desperately hopeful. "Are you sure?" he finally asked.

"Yes," Gabriel promised, squeezing his hand. "I thought you knew. I mean, I know female omegas aren't the same but..." he must have seen the doubt in Ray's eyes, "You can ask Alec."

"I..." Ray leaned back further until the wall at his back was supporting his weight because suddenly he didn't feel so light anymore, just light-headed. Just *stupid*, just a stupid, selfish coward. Because he'd never learned these things, he'd figured they weren't his problem. But Gabriel had. Gabriel, who'd been so cold since he'd become Ray's mate compared to how fun he'd been when they'd just been cousins, had bothered to find out what would happen to his mate. And Ray never had. "I never thought..." he tried to explain.

And Gabriel nodded, interpreting Ray's words as positively as could be. "You thought you'd be an alpha." He slowly raised his other hand to cup Ray's elbow and rub it slowly.

Ray nodded weakly. It wasn't what he'd meant, but it was true. Even if the idea felt almost absurd now, like a childish dream instead of what he'd been taught all his life to expect for himself.

"I'm sorry, Ray." Gabriel leaned in closer, embracing him fully and murmuring in his ear in that careful voice, like he was afraid that if he spoke too loudly or too fast Ray would break. Ray remembered that voice, remembered being scared and finding comfort in it. "I should have realised nobody had told you how it works for omegas." Ray wasn't even sure he was mistaken, that he *wouldn't* break, not the way he could feel himself trembling, the relief as shocking as the fear. "It's going to be okay, really. You'll have time to get used to it," Gabriel continued and Ray let his head fall forward, let Gabriel take some of his weight. His scent was familiar. Safe. If he was allowed, Ray just wanted to stay close a little longer. Just until he was needed.

He just needed to know one thing first. "How much time?"

He felt Gabriel swallow against his cheek, stubble rasping softly against his own hairless skin. "A couple months, it... it depends on a lot of things, really. Alec explained it to us."

"Why didn't he explain it to me?" Ray demanded angrily. But he wasn't angry, not really. He was *hurt*.

Gabriel just kept petting him, like he couldn't hear Ray's anger, or like he could tell what lay underneath it. "He said you freaked out when he tried to talk to you about it."

Fuck. It was true, and he knew Alec was afraid of him. Or maybe of hurting him, but he definitely didn't feel like he could speak freely. It wasn't Alec's fault Ray was an omega, but it'd been so easy to make him shut up about it. He'd said he wanted to know, but with everything that he couldn't ignore, it'd been so hard to listen to even more.

He hadn't realised some of the news might be good.

H e hadn't apologized, exactly, but he'd admitted that he hadn't been open to listening before.

Alec had nodded, still looking uncertain and checked once more, "And now you are? Because I don't want to make you listen any more than..." he trailed off, but Ray thought he knew what he meant: any more than he wanted to force Ray to have sex with him.

And he hadn't. He'd offered to walk away. He'd offered to stay. Ray had simply been too scared of the alternative to tell him what he truly wanted. "I am," he said, not sure he was telling the truth but willing himself to be.

According to Alec, he'd have at least three months—maybe up to five since it'd been a large litter—before his mating heats would return. "It'll still be the full moon, you'll feel it. We all will, but we might end up hunting bunnies in the woods for all I know. Mating won't be a priority."

"So you can't promise it won't happen," Ray pointed out, shifting Clara's weight as she nursed. Of all the alphas, Alec seemed the most immune to the sight and Ray liked to have someone else to focus on while they talked about this.

"No, but even if... Ray, sex doesn't always mean knotting, you know that. And anyway, the chances of conceiving while lactating are extremely low."

"Wait, what?" He looked up from his daughter. "So I should... I should keep doing it? You said I could stop after a month."

"You can," Alec replied. "But... yes, it'd improve your chances of not conceiving."

Ray's stomach was twisted into knots and he had to exhale carefully to keep himself calm—a nursing baby was bound to react badly if he got upset. "But the sex... I don't need it?"

Alec's face fell. "We need it, to feel close to you, to..." He looked down. "Heats will come back, yes, and you will need sex then, and when it's been long enough they'll get... stronger."

And Ray didn't need a dictionary: they'd get strong enough that breeding would be the only viable alternative.

But not right away.

Ray stepped back and flopped down into one of the rocking chairs, setting it creaking as he stared into space. Clara grumbled a little, but quickly settled, not much caring as long as the food kept coming. "That's..."

"Good, I hope? I had no idea you wouldn't know about this, I swear."

"No, I know," Ray glanced at him, "I know, it's just that I..." Ray snorted, exhaling wetly. Once, then again, and finally he was collected enough to speak. "I thought..."

"You thought it was going to happen again right away," Alec said softly.

"Yeah," he admitted. "I thought they'd be horrible if I didn't have sex, everybody says that omegas need sex."

"Well, our bodies are a little smarter than that. How many pups would survive to adulthood if their main caretaker was so exhausted they couldn't stay awake?"

Ray was tired—what with his on and off sleeping—so he didn't manage to quite repress his flinch and Alec saw it. He came over and knelt by Ray's feet, like he thought he was a knight or something. He didn't touch Ray, though. He didn't have the confidence to. "Scientifically, it won't be like that with us. We'll help you."

Ray exhaled, feeling stupid for asking but *needing it*. "And you won't..."

"We will put it off as long as we can," Alec promised fiercely, then put one of his hands near Ray's thigh on the sofa. An offer, not an imposition. Ray eyed it warily but hopefully: Maybe they could make it work. But it couldn't be one-sided.

"I'm sorry I've been... difficult to talk to," he told Alec. "I figured that if I didn't know. I don't know, that it wouldn't happen. It was stupid."

"It's natural, this is all new to you, and... you didn't even expect it."

And just then the other question that had been rounding Ray's mind popped up, and this time, he asked it, "Could I have done something? To... to be an alpha?"

It was Alec who looked away then, swallowing and hunching his shoulders, tense like... He shook his head and with effort looked up into Ray's eyes. "I don't really know. Nobody... We... it's pretty much impossible to tell without testing with live subjects, and nobody wants to do that. We could do twin studies, you know, reared together and apart, but nobody would *do that*, not when the kids are werewolves."

Ray was silent. He hadn't expected that. He'd thought that if he managed to ask, he'd at least *know*. Maybe Alec could tell how lost he was feeling, because he finally found the courage to put his hands on Ray's knees, just resting them there. Ray could have pushed them away, or moved his legs. Alec would have probably fallen on his arse to get away from him. He didn't. Alec started speaking again. "I asked Gabriel about you, I... to understand you better, because I always say the wrong thing."

Ray glance up at him, surprised. He'd noticed Alec's tenderness with the pups, with him in the den, but he hadn't realised it was *planned*. "He said your dad passed when you were young," Alec continued, watching Ray closely for a reaction. "That you'd always helped your mum a lot with your younger siblings. That they followed you around like you'd invented solid ground. And that could have been an alpha, easy. A leader."

"But...?" Ray asked when he paused too long.

"But nothing, it wasn't, it was an omega, a caretaker... a leader, too. Just a different type."

Ray snorted and turned his body away. It didn't dislodge Alec's hands—Ray couldn't move far with Clara on his lap—but he had been right: Alec pulled away.

"Ray," Alec insisted. "You got veto power. You will decide who can be part of the pack and who can't. You will know where everybody in the pack is, you will—"

"I will do what my First Alpha tells me," Ray interrupted between gritted teeth.

"So will I," Alec pointed out, breathing a little fast but keeping his voice even.

Ray swallowed, annoyed because he was right and upset because it didn't really change anything for *Ray*. He'd never expected to be First Alpha, he hadn't even bragged about the possibility like some boys did. Maybe, deep down, he'd always known. He tapped Alec's elbow, signalling he wanted out and his lover sprung to his feet.

And then they were standing, eye to eye, the baby between them asleep. "I know you didn't offer to be my shrink," he told Alec, "and it's not that I don't appreciate it, but... I'm kinda fucked up." He pointed at his own head with his free hand.

"I did offer," Alec corrected, green eyes on his. "I'm your alpha, that means I offered you everything."

"In exchange for the same?"

Alec shook his head, sadly and little angrily, Ray thought. "Not in exchange, it's just yours, if you want it."

"I—" Ray started, and then the cry pierced the air. They both tensed, heads tilting to better identify the sound. Ray sighed, in relief and tiredness both: Jamie was hungry.

When he turned back to Alec, he found an apologetic smile on his lips—like he couldn't help the fondness, but he regretted James' constant hunger. Ray could have sympathized with that, but then Alec apologized, "I'm sorry about him, I know he's a bit of a pain."

Ray froze, swallowing his anger, torn between his need to go to Jamie—who was a bit of a pain but was *his* pain—and his need to snap at Jamie's father. "Me too," he said instead, and Alec's eyes widened. "But I don't think we should start apologizing for our kid's existence this early, even if it *is* a British tradition."

Alec blinked, and then his mouth curved into a smile that Ray almost wanted to kiss.

And then Jamie cried out again and he had to look away and go.

He didn't want apologies, Ray decided, cradling his son in his arms, feeling the insistent pull of his mouth on his tit. You couldn't build a future thinking of what you'd done wrong in the past. Maybe he could have done something to be an alpha, but he hadn't. What he had now was this warm body against his, and all the others of his pack. He wasn't where he had expected and he wasn't sure where he was going; but wherever that was, he wasn't alone.

[End book I]

Simpler Than Most (a romance)

The Stars of the Pack – Book I.I

Blurb

Sergi has stopped lying to himself: he's had a crush on a guy for a while. Things seem to be looking up when the guy turns out to be an omega and he agrees to take Sergi as his bondmate. But it isn't as simple as alpha meets omega and they live happily ever after.

For one thing, Ray has four other alphas. For another, one of them seems intent on ignoring every one of the conventions alphas are meant to live by. Sergi should be angry and he's certainly worried, but the more lines Iesu crosses, the closer he gets to the person Sergi has always been afraid to be.

Is Sergi brave enough to face himself and does Iesu have the patience to wait him out while he does?

[An interlude in The Stars of the Pack series]

Thanks to Alna, for the title and all the great feedback. Toni and Dana, for making sure I don't forget any words. And everyone who has reviewed other books, or let me know what they liked. Hope you enjoy this peek behind the scenes!

Prologue

"So, are we going to do something about it?"

Sergi looked up from the cement he was laying down on a line of bricks and glanced around, trying to figure out if they'd messed something up. Gabriel had given them the easiest job he could because neither of them had any experience with construction. There was nothing out of place, Iesu had completed about as much of the next layer of bricks as he could—neat and straight like their foreman had asked. "About what?"

"This crush you have on me," Iesu said. Except he couldn't have. Sergi stared at him, hoping the words would start making sense. Iesu still had a bit of an accent and sometimes he'd use strange words—not wrong, really, just not quite the ones Sergi expected.

"What?" he said again when Iesu didn't rephrase or repeat.

The other alpha wasn't smiling for once, but his lips were still slightly curved upwards as if on the cusp of laughter. And Sergi probably shouldn't have noticed that. Iesu sighed, then took another brick and placed it precisely right, pressing it slightly against the cement underneath. He was relaxed, heartbeat steady and unrushed. And then he did repeat it, equally unbothered. "This crush you have on me. I just

121

wondered if you were planning on ever acting on it." At that, he glanced up at Sergi through his dark eyelashes, not in defiance, but... Was that a challenge? Did he want to fight?

"Are you crazy?" he blurted out, too shocked for politeness. "Why... I don't..." He stopped talking and Iesu straightened at once, dark eyes sharply attentive.

"You don't have a crush on me?" he inquired very politely, but it was a dare, of course. Because if Sergi said it and it wasn't true, they both knew his body would give away the lie.

And it was stupid because Iesu *knew*. And he wasn't acting anything like Sergi had imagined. He wasn't freaking out and he wasn't punching him. But none of that meant it wasn't crazy. "Just... stop. I don't know what you expect to accomplish with this, but—"

"Orgasms," Iesu interrupted. It was against protocol, and combined with the rest of this absurd conversation, enough insult to throw the first punch. But Sergi was too confused to be angry. He gaped at Iesu for long enough the other alpha had the chance to continue, "I thought you told Ray you had grown enough balls to admit you liked guys; what's the holdup now?"

"I like *Ray*," Sergi almost spat. He glared down at the cement. Too thick and too quick-drying to be left unfinished, he had to at least finish the layer so Iesu could put the bricks down or it'd dry like that and ruin the whole thing. They barely had enough money to get the materials, which was why they were doing all the work themselves. If they delayed the project, Gabriel would probably kill them both.

"And you like me," Iesu calmly repeated. "I can tell: you keep looking at my chest when I take my shirt off."

Sergi glared at him. Why did he even *do* that? It was winter; it didn't matter how hard they worked, it wasn't enough to make them sweat through their clothes. Iesu said he was used to the cold because he'd only come to England when he was ten, but Romania had milder winters than England and Iesu was a werewolf, so he couldn't feel the effects of the weather that keenly in any case. Of course Sergi had stared: the guy had got half naked in the middle of their work day for no logical reason! "Yeah, sure, because Romania is cold, right? Like I don't know where Romania is or can't google what the temperature is like!"

That shut Iesu up, but not for long, and when he spoke, Sergi realised his mistake. "You looked up the weather in Romania?"

Sergi shrugged, painstakingly evening out yet another half meter of grey paste. "You kept talking about it. Not like googling is hard."

"No," Iesu admitted. "What's the weather like in Russia?"

"What?"

"Isn't that where your mum is from?" Iesu asked. He leaned closer to the bricks, presumably to make sure they were properly aligned, but with vision in the range of 200/20, he'd only need to lean that close to solder on microchips.

He also couldn't quite see how they'd gone from accusing him of having a crush on another alpha to talking about his mother's origins, but he'd take the out if it was offered. "Yeah, but she came over when she was little. Her pack was struggling, and she had an aunt here."

He didn't mean to look up, but he still caught Iesu's sympathetic grimace. "Yeah, not even the land is enough, what with humans—" He cut himself off and shook his head, as if dislodging the unpleasant thoughts. Sergi wasn't surprised: from what he'd seen, Iesu didn't seem capable of taking much seriously. He only realised he was still looking when the other man raised his head and met his eyes. "So, do you speak Russian?"

"Oh, not really. A few phrases, but..." He shrugged. "She didn't want my dad to feel left out."

"Oh, that sucks," Iesu said sympathetically, then randomly offered, "I like the Cyrillic alphabet."

Sergi frowned at him. He liked the sound of his mother's language, but the alphabet gave him a headache with all the letters that looked the same as English but were actually pronounced differently. "Shouldn't you hate Russians?"

"Because of something that happened forty years before I was born?" Iesu asked. He only spared Sergi a glance in between laying his bricks. "Not really. It's hardly people's fault that their leaders suck. The Russians didn't even choose them democratically."

"Do you like history?" he asked, mostly because he was afraid of what Iesu would come up with if left to his own devices.

"It's sad," Iesu said thoughtfully. "But... yeah, I could never stop myself from listening in class. Like a train wreck, you know? Can't look away."

"It's not all sad," Sergi pointed out. Even when it was, at least it was certain. The past couldn't change. He had liked history in school, and he'd almost taken it for A levels, but his teachers had known he didn't want to go to university, so he'd ended up doing DT instead. "And at least you know, it's done. And you can learn from it and avoid it."

"Is it?" Iesu asked mildly, lining up another brick "I don't think so; we find out new stuff all the time. Plus, it depends who tells you the story."

"Well, yes, victors and all, but still, there's evidence—"

"There's a lot of evidence that we don't learn anything," Iesu said, interrupting once again.

Sergi was quiet, surprised but not offended. "What's got into you? You're normally so..." He waved, not quite sure of what word to use. Iesu was downright cheery most of the time. In Sergi's experience, it was almost impossible to get him to drop the smile.

"Optimistic?" Iesu offered with a wry smile.

"Yeah," he said, but looked down at his work. He wasn't sure this was that much better than talk about crushes.

Iesu laughed, but it was nothing like his usual joyful laughter. It sounded bitter. "Not really; I'm just happy. I know it doesn't last, so I enjoy it."

That made Sergi smile despite himself. "That's... incredibly dark, actually." He didn't mean to glance up either.

"Yeah, well, the whole point of carpe diem is that you gotta seize the day because it will *end*," he said this while watching Sergi's face pointedly. Was he...? He licked his lips. "Wanna seize the day with me?" he asked with mischief in his eyes.

Sergi snorted. Iesu might have been kidding, but it was such a bad pickup line... "Are we jumping off a bridge?"

Iesu put down the brick in his hands and straightened, meeting Sergi's eyes full on. He had dark brown eyes, framed by lashes they'd have put on ads for mascara. He was wearing a shirt today, but it didn't matter: he was beautiful, and he was looking straight at Sergi like he wanted to devour him. "Depends, are you going to hold my hand?"

Sergi swallowed, torn between everything he knew should happen in a situation such as this and everything that was actually going on through his head. Through his body: his heart was racing, his skin flushing, he was... "You are serious...?"

Iesu just nodded, pulse a little faster now, but steady. The guy had balls of *steel*. "Yes, I'm serious. I want you."

The words seemed to cut through Sergi's defences, leaving him shaky and uncertain. He could say no, he knew. If he did, it'd be safe; everything would go back to normal. Iesu would still know the truth, but he was hardly going to tell anybody, was he? Maybe he was actually more pessimistic than Sergi had assumed, but he wasn't a dick to go and tell on Sergi because Sergi had rejected him.

Nobody would know. Except them. The idea of actually leaving it hanging between them was almost worse. The only thing worse than being afraid was being afraid in front of someone who was brave. Except Iesu didn't seem to care enough to need to be brave—it sounded like he could take it or leave it. He was interested enough to ask, but not worried enough about Sergi's reaction to be truly nervous.

Iesu sighed. "What about a kiss?" he asked gently, and his pulse picked up. "Trial run, you are satisfied, or you get your money back."

Sergi didn't get this guy: he'd been cool as a cucumber asking for orgasms, but he was getting all nervous over a kiss? Except that left him with zero excuses: Iesu wanted him and he was willing to not just ask but insist. He had to care at least a little.

And Sergi could be the coward who passed up on something they both knew very well he wanted, or he could... His eyes dropped to Iesu's lips and he snatched them away as fast as he could. But of course, Iesu had seen. He could hardly miss it the way he was staring at Sergi's face, so intent it almost felt like he was trying to read his mind. Sergi glanced around, unconsciously looking for witnesses. Or an excuse.

But he didn't *want* an excuse. He hadn't lied to Ray: he had been awful to him because he couldn't deal with being attracted to another man, and he'd also grown the fuck up and got over it. Back when he'd hit Ray over the head with that ball to get his attention, there was no way in hell he'd been able to walk up to Josh and tell him he was interested in joining the new pack. It was fine for an alpha to want a male omega, but Sergi had been all too conscious that his preference had nothing to do with pheromones and the moon.

Male omegas weren't an exception to him. It hadn't been just Ray. And it wasn't just Ray now.

He met Iesu's eyes again, gave a tiny nod. The other alpha's face broke into a smile, glad and joyful. Sergi could see what he'd said in his face: the way he honestly relished every little thing.

He stepped around the half-built wall slowly, as if afraid of frightening a skittish horse. Sergi just stood there, fists clenched and breath coming out too fast. And then Iesu stopped right in front of him, too close but not quite stepping into his personal space. His smile was teasing this time, and he licked his full bottom lip before speaking, effectively making sure Sergi missed the first half of his sentence. "...spin the bottle."

He looked up and saw in Iesu's dimples that his distraction had been noted. He bit down on a question and stepped forward instead, taking hold of Iesu's upper arm hard enough to make the other man straighten up, eyes widening. Iesu's lips parted to speak and Sergi leaned in and stopped him with his mouth. He pressed his lips against Iesu's, moving them slowly but firmly. He wasn't backing down now.

It wasn't like kissing Ray had been at all. Of course, he was neither moon high nor fucking his new omega, so it was a rather absurd comparison. His wolf was turned on, just like he was, but Sergi was most definitely the one in charge.

And he was kissing a man. He hadn't really thought of it that way when it'd been Ray—maybe because all his wolf cared about was the fact that Ray was an omega. *Their* omega.

Iesu made a sound in his mouth and Sergi took the chance to push his tongue past his lips. Iesu sucked on it and Sergi realised his hands were around Iesu's neck, tilting his face so he could kiss him deeper. He tasted like the tomato and oregano pasta sauce Alec had made for lunch. Like home, like... There were hands on his own clothes, tugging at his shirt hard enough to make him stumble forward and press them together from clavicle to knee. It sent a pulse of heat through Sergi's cock and made him thrust. Iesu growled and tugged harder, trying to pull him closer, and that was when his own dick, equally hard and ready, pressed against Sergi's leg. Sergi tripped over his own two feet when he stumbled back—only Iesu's grip kept him from falling on his arse.

But Iesu had felt it because he let go and took a step back. His skin was flushed, his eyes dark and round, and he smelled of sweat, sunlight and sex. Sergi watched him warily, heart beating ten miles an hour and body all out of sorts. A part of him wanted to step closer again, feel the warmth of the other alpha's body against him, against his cock, which was most unhappy that Sergi had interrupted the good times...

But he couldn't move. His body wasn't the problem—he'd tried not to think about it too much, but he'd jerked off to guys before. He had... He had known the attraction was real, that they could make his body react. But he'd thought it'd be physical. In fact, he had pictured it just like heat: an uncontrollable urge he had to satisfy, an unthinking impulse he couldn't stop, even if he wanted to.

Thinking back on it, he didn't feel so great about fucking Ray on the ground, about the way he hadn't even asked if Ray was okay or needed him to do something different. But the moon didn't know how to be gentle; it just wasn't its nature.

It hadn't been up to Sergi and he knew perfectly well he'd do it again. It was a truth he understood to his very core: he could not resist an omega in heat any more than he could resist the tide.

This was nothing like that. He'd stepped back. Just because he'd felt Iesu's cock against his leg, nothing more, not even a little pain. All it had taken to stop him in his tracks had been another man's erection and that was all in his head. That was on him. His wolf wasn't scared, or freaked, or shaking a little. He knew it wasn't the wolf because the wolf didn't hesitate or doubt.

Iesu held his gaze a moment longer—a strange perversion of an alpha stand-off—and then shook his head and turned away, effectively conceding. Except there was nothing to concede. This wasn't a fight. This was... Sergi didn't know what it was, except wrong.

It sounded a little pathetic when put like that, but it also meant whatever happened was Sergi's responsibility. If he did this, he'd have no excuses to hide behind. "I... I mean, we can't. Ray—"

Iesu straightened. "What?" he said. He'd lost his easy-going nature like someone shedding a cloak. Sergi could almost smell his anger now, like something burning, and he suddenly looked dangerous. Like an alpha, like a predator.

"Well, it's cheating. We are not—"

"Oh, for fuck's sake," Iesu spat. "Ray would *thank us* if we found ourselves a way not to bother him."

"He—" Sergi tried to say.

"He's tired, as anyone would be," Iesu snapped. "Just because he can have five mates, it doesn't mean it's easy. So, if you are not interested, just ask to take it back, no harm done. I told you before. But do *not* bullshit me."

"Okay, I—"

But Iesu didn't let him finish, he turned around and headed for the house. "Finish the goddamned wall on your own. I'm going to check if Ray needs anything."

Chapter 1

T he craziest thing was that he didn't act any differently around Sergi the next time he saw him. And the next time he saw him was at dinner that night. They were having take-away because Alec had taken a shift at the closest hospital and wouldn't get back till late. Gabriel had pretty much decided on his own that they should focus on the house at the moment, but Alec made enough money with any work he did that it was well worth letting him work instead of trying to teach him to make brick walls. Sergi tried not to resent it; after all, the guy had spent *years* cramming to be a doctor and it was obviously the only reason he'd got to be in the pack in the first place. He was the shyest alpha Sergi had ever met, for one, and even though he was the second oldest, he'd let everyone else go before him when they'd mated Ray for the first time.

Nothing like Iesu, who could have probably charmed Ray into dating him if he'd wanted to. Not that men in their pack dated other men, of course. A friend could give you a hand here and there—mostly during the full-moon—and some guys got more enthusiastic than others about it. But that was it. Guys liked sex, and sometimes it was convenient to have sex with other guys.

Iesu's idea wasn't that crazy, really, when he thought about it like that. Except it was meant to be *convenient*, not... You weren't meant to want it enough that a kiss got you hard in less than five minutes.

And that had always been the problem. Sergi had never managed to think about it the right way; somehow, he hadn't been able to keep his mind on other things—on girls—when the possibility had come up.

So he hadn't done it. It was easier that way; if he wasn't doing it at all, he couldn't be... gay. And anyway, he loved women; their soft bodies and rising laughter, the glint of challenge in their eyes when they asked to be chased—literally or metaphorically.

He just didn't want Iesu to be angry with him and make things weird. They were in the same pack now and that pack was only six persons big—it wasn't like they could avoid each other. And of all the alphas, Iesu was the easiest to spend time with—relaxed and fun, and with unexpected depths even before he'd started going on about history repeating itself. Ray had apparently liked him a little before but other than that, he hadn't known him well like Josh and Gabriel, so it didn't feel like he had an unfair advantage.

Not that it was a competition, he wasn't an idiot. None of them were going anywhere, and it was obvious that Ray wasn't taking well to being an omega—he didn't have time to have a favourite. Iesu was probably right and he'd prefer it if they distracted themselves somehow. Not that Sergi needed to sleep with someone else for that, he had plenty of work and plenty to keep him distracted when he wasn't at work. He wasn't going to stop seeing his family and his friends in their old pack, after all, only now he had to run for half an hour to get around the river to see them.

It took a promise to owe her a big favour, but Irina agreed to drive him to the closest art store to buy the supplies Ray's mother had suggested he'd like, and even to drive him back home so he wouldn't have to carry the canvases back on two legs.

By the time he made it upstairs to Gabriel's guest room, he was starting to question whether he was going to be making an arse of himself in front of the guy he wanted to impress. But he'd done it already, and he was sure it'd make Ray happy, so what if he looked desperate? It wasn't like Ray liked him anyway. Sergi knew he'd probably only agreed to take him in because his uncle had required he take no less than five alphas as mates, and he'd been too close to his first heat to think clearly.

But he could show him he'd made the right choice. He had been trying to prove himself to Ray since they had been boys, and now that he'd come right out and told him that, what sense did it make to hold back?

"Ray?" he called out. He didn't have any free hands to knock.

Ray took a little longer than someone with supernatural reflexes should have needed, and Sergi's stomach fell. He could tell Ray was inside. But that didn't mean he wanted to see Sergi, of course. Maybe he didn't want to see *anybody*, but Sergi couldn't help but suspect—

The door opened. Ray was in soft-looking pyjamas, looking sleepy and relaxed. And miserable. It was impossible to miss the slope of his shoulders and the defeated cast of his chin. He blinked at Sergi as if slowly processing what he was seeing, then frowned. "Is that... Is that a canvas?"

"Um, yeah. I got your art supplies?" he offered as he glanced down at his own arms. He'd loved Ray's paintings for years, but he couldn't have guessed what he used to create them, so he'd gone to the source to ask. It turned out Ray hadn't even taken his oils or brushes from his mother's. She'd insisted he return them to their owner and advised him regarding what canvases to purchase.

Ray stepped forward and took one of the bags off his wrist, immediately glancing inside. "These are..."

"Your mum gave them to me," Sergi explained a little warily. He hadn't considered that Ray might feel territorial about his things. Sergi didn't much care if people touched his stuff, but some wolves thought of the objects they owned as part of their territory and got twitchy if someone touched them. Not that Sergi had really done anything to them; Ray's mum had packed it up and he'd just carried in plastic bags, surely...

"Fuck, you..." Ray glanced up, and Sergi realised he wasn't angry. In fact, he was *smiling*. "Did you see them?"

"See them?" Sergi asked, smiling back automatically. Ray's blue eyes were shining. It was probably the first time he'd seen him smile from up close. "Your mother made me stay for lunch and give her an update! She's worried sick, but she doesn't want to walk into your territory when you don't even have a territory yet."

Ray was clearly surprised at that. Sergi couldn't blame the guy; he'd had enough dropped on his plate without worrying about everybody else's reactions. "What did you tell her?" he asked. He was trying to be casual as he unpacked the supplies, but of course, he couldn't hide his body from Sergi's keen senses.

He was almost sorry to intrude, even if he couldn't help it. He shrugged. "The truth: that you are bored." He tapped the case of brushes meaningfully before handing them over to Ray. "And lonely and freaked out," he added, making sure to keep his tone steady. He was a little nervous, but he was always a little uncomfortable around Ray—that hadn't changed just because Ray was his mate now. And he wasn't lying, even if maybe he was wrong. "But that with a little time, you'll be fine," he promised. "And then you'll call her, and of course, she and your siblings will be welcome in our territory any time."

Ray hesitated, glancing around restlessly. "You seem very sure of that," he said after a pause. He clearly wasn't so sure himself. Again, Sergi couldn't really complain. It had been hard enough for him to admit he liked Ray. *Men.* To present omega and have a male partner become the only choice... No, not just that. To have your alpha demand that you take multiple mates and form a pack? If it had been Sergi, he'd have been rocking back and forth in a corner. Ray looked like he was tempted, but he'd kept it together so far—Sergi was damn impressed.

He met Ray's eyes. He knew it was hard to believe, but Sergi did believe it. Believe in him. He knew how strong Ray was, and if he'd ever doubted it, his resilience in the face of the shitty cards he'd been dealt would have been more than enough. He didn't know how to say it so Ray would believe him, though.

"I spent a lot of time fighting with you," he said in the end. "I figure I know what you're made of by now."

He couldn't tell if Ray believed him, but sometimes all you could do was offer your faith. Again, and again, a prayer and an offering, and hope someone was listening.

The house was going well enough—Gabriel had said they'd finish it with enough time for Ray to come live there right before the babies were born. Sergi had never seen a new pack forming around a First Omega before, and there were a lot of ceremonies he'd never even heard of and didn't see much sense to, but having the First Omega's birth blood soak into the new territory did make a lot of sense. Blood and magic always went together—it was like everything non-magical in the world, really; you didn't get anything for free.

Still, it was also pretty freaky so he was happy to take a holiday from working at the local supermarket to look after his completely made-up elderly aunt so he could get his mate a nice, cosy place to live in when he finished giving birth for the first time. He was trying not to think of the babies too much, he had younger cousins and he'd changed his fair share of diapers, but that was different than being a *father*.

He couldn't imagine how he'd feel when he actually held a baby in his arms that was *his*. It was crazy enough how obsessed his wolf was with having Ray close... and closer. He'd always liked sex but now he *needed it*. It didn't seem right to ask for it—not when Ray was visibly struggling with the pregnancy and clearly couldn't be less in the mood—but Alec had explained it was normal. The wolves apparently needed to keep fucking their mate even now he was carrying their children. No, *especially* because he was carrying their children. It was probably a mechanism to make sure the alpha wolves stuck around to protect their omega while he was vulnerable.

Well done, Mother Nature, Sergi thought bitterly as he dragged his eyes away from Ray's exposed collarbone like a medieval monk seeing a woman for the first time in years.

Ray offered him a tired smile when he caught him staring, seeming to assume Sergi was looking at his drawing, and he had to get up and make up an excuse to leave.

Chapter 2

Iesu blinked up at him from where he was sitting on the couch with his family. The TV was on to something with a lot of swearing, even though at least three of the people huddled around the television were young kids. He got a few looks, but everyone considerably more worried about Iesu's mother blocking the TV on her way back to her seat, so he got to stand there like a dolt until Iesu got to his feet, already rolling his eyes. "Shameless," he explained. "Good to pick up English, apparently."

He gestured towards the door, and Sergi retraced his steps to the little foyer full of umbrellas, shoes, and coats. Iesu closed the living room door behind them and leaned against it. He was relaxed and easy, not bothering to straighten up to his full height, so confident he didn't need to be taller or look ready to attack. He just wasn't afraid.

Not that he had anything to be afraid of, Sergi realised, but it was just... expected. You gave other alphas respect by showing them you considered them a threat.

"Everything okay?" he checked, and Sergi realised he'd been silent too long.

"Yeah!" he said, feeling a little guilty. He could barely hold back an apology. He glanced around, calculating the odds of being overheard.

"TV's on loud," Iesu commented. "You can talk."

"What if I don't want to talk?" he bit out, and then clamped his mouth shut as his pulse skyrocketed in terror.

"You— You don't?" Iesu asked, his heartbeat picking up in turn. Good, at least Sergi wasn't the only one freaking out.

Sergi shook his head. "I'm just... My wolf keeps pulling at me, but I don't want..."

"To feel like you have to think of England the entire time?"

He shrugged. "He needs more time, and I figured..." He risked a glance. Iesu could hardly get offended when he'd propositioned Sergi himself, but he could say no, and then... Well, he'd have to go to Ray and ask him because he'd been so turned on all the time for the last three days, he was afraid to go anywhere near a power tool, and he knew all too well how that would turn out when the full moon rose. Or when his wolf snapped—whichever came first.

And he could hardly blame Iesu for refusing; he might have been pretty chill about protocol, but that didn't mean Sergi's rejection hadn't hurt.

"Okay."

Sergi's head snapped up, and he met Iesu's eyes. "Okay?"

Iesu was already licking his lips. "Sure, do you trust the TV, or do you want to go to my car?"

Sergi hesitated. He didn't even know what would happen if they got found out. Alphas got off together during the full moon all the time and nobody cared. But then again, they did call it being moon-mad... Still, he wanted at least the illusion of some privacy if he was going to do this. "TV. I mean, your room?"

Iesu gave a nod, then leaned closer. He didn't touch Sergi, though, instead, he got a key off the hook by the door. "Back door," he explained with a smirk. He'd heard Sergi startle, then, and he could probably tell he was halfway to hard already.

All pack houses were built in sight of each other but with about a hundred meters in between them to give them all a little privacy despite their enhanced senses. There were people around other gardens—their laughter and bickering carried with the sound of cicadas in the night air—but nobody in sight as they made their way around the house. The family must have all been in the TV room because Iesu led the way up the stairs without slowing down, and Sergi—he couldn't help but listen—didn't hear anyone moving upstairs.

Iesu's room was in the attic, it turned out, which meant he could only really stand straight in the very centre of the room. He admitted that with a shrug and warned Sergi not to knock himself out, then explained, "One word: *privacy*."

"What do you need a room for when a car will do the job?" Sergi asked, and it came out a little snarkier than he meant to. Sue him, he was nervous.

Iesu shot him a look and laughed, deep and rich, and as far as he could tell, completely honest. "Well, sometimes I like to take my time," he said and took off his t-shirt a little more slowly than he needed to.

Not that Sergi could complain. His mouth was dry and he... he had come here for this, hadn't he?

He only realised he'd been watching the other alpha's abs when Iesu took a step back and plopped down on the double bed dominating the room. The sheets were mussed, and gazing at him from under his eyelashes like that, Iesu looked like he had just woken up.

And not from dreaming of electric sheep, either.

He swallowed, wetting his lips even as his words got stoppered up in his throat.

"So what hang-ups are we going to avoid here?" Iesu asked, stretching like a cat, his skin looking tanned against the white bedding, luminescent in the low light of the standing lamp.

"What?"

"Are you going to let me kiss you on the mouth?" he asked, smirking. He could tell Sergi was having trouble keeping his eyes off his chest.

He growled, frustrated, with Iesu and himself and his stupid cock—all too happy to get started when Sergi's mind was all over the place. "No hang-ups," he snapped and crawled up the bed and sat right on the bulge tenting the other alpha's jeans. It was *hot*, and he...

But Iesu inhaled like he'd been punched, and his hands clenched on empty air a second before Sergi's hands landed on his wrists and ground them down onto the bed. "What about you?" he challenged. "Anything I need to know?"

Iesu's eyes shone brightly and his smile was like a bite. "Nope," he said and licked his lips. "I can take it."

So Sergi leaned in and kissed him, not just passionate—he couldn't hold that back no matter what—but biting. He wanted to devour him, suck on his tongue until Iesu begged him to suck elsewhere, fuck his mouth until he asked for that too. Iesu arched up under him, pressing his erection against Sergi's arse, but this time he was ready.

More than ready; he'd spent the last two weeks fantasizing about feeling that weight against him again. Only it wasn't quite... He transferred Iesu's wrist to his right hand—he couldn't have held him if Iesu had struggled, but all the other man did was use the better leverage to push his tongue into Sergi's own mouth.

Sergi sucked on it, scrabbling at Iesu's jeans for an embarrassingly long time before he got his fingers to unhook the button and lower the zipper. That distracted Iesu into a groan that interrupted the kiss, and when Sergi pushed his hand inside his underwear and pulled out Iesu's cock, he buckled hard enough he almost managed to send Sergi rolling off the bed.

"Sorry," he mumbled, hooking a leg behind Sergi's knee. He tugged on Sergi's hold, apparently happy to pretend he couldn't pull out of it any time he liked. "You too," he demanded, glancing down between their bodies. There were spots of colour on his cheeks and chest, nipples rosy and peaked. It seemed weird they'd taste like salt and skin when Sergi ignored him and leaned in to suck one into his mouth.

Iesu moaned, too loud and almost tortured, and Sergi got harder in his own trousers. But he wanted... He moved to the left nipple. Iesu yanked his right hand from his grip and before he knew it, he'd taken Sergi's face in his hand and brought him up into a kiss so filthy it seemed crazy he was dressed for it. He wasn't for long, anyway: Iesu took care of his trousers fast—clearly a good multitasker—and then tried to gather both their cocks into his hand. He grunted, frustrated when he couldn't manage it.

It was just not happening; Iesu's hand would have had to be disproportionately big for it to work. He lowered his hips, pressing his dick right against the soft trail down Iesu's belly and nestling his cock against the other alpha's.

"Oh, *fuck*," Iesu swore, voice thready and desperate, and shifted his hips to get them aligned, then tugged at his still-captive hand. "Lemme..."

Sergi let him go, bending his elbows to push them close from neck to groin. His own nipples felt on fire under his t-shirt. He shivered, wishing he'd taken it off too. He guided Iesu's face right into another kiss, too wet and uncoordinated because they were both too busy pushing their cocks together in the sweaty, sticky mess they'd created between their bodies.

He was so... Iesu used the foot he'd hooked behind his knee to thrust even harder and Sergi shuddered so hard he thought he'd lose his balance. But he was safe anyway, Iesu had an arm around his waist and the nails of his other hand digging so deep into Sergi's arm that if he could smell anything but sweat and precome, it'd have been his own blood.

"Come on," Iesu demanded, panting desperately into his mouth. "*Harder*."

Sergi laughed and shoved his hips down hard enough he'd bruise where he'd hit Iesu's hip bone. His lover growled, shoving right back at him, and the feeling of his cock sliding against his own sent what felt like a shot of lightning up Sergi's spine. He pushed harder and faster, again, and once more after and he was *done*. He kept moving even as he made a right mess between them, too much come, and holding too hard onto Iesu's hair so he could kiss his stupid red lips as his body and brain simply stopped—too overwhelmed for time to register.

He slumped forward, shaky and panting like crazy.

Iesu groaned, shifting under him, and Sergi realised with a start that he hadn't come. "Fuck, sorry," he said at once. This he didn't mind apologizing for. "Let—"

But Iesu didn't; he used his hold on Sergi's waist to flip them with a neat twist of his hips that squashed their trapped cocks between them for an endless instant of white hot pleasure-pain and ended up with Iesu laying on top of him, kissing him hard enough to draw blood and shoving against his navel like he wanted to spear him through.

He made a sound that wanted to be a word right next to Sergi's ear and Sergi twisted his neck to capture his mouth. The kiss he got was sloppy, but it gave him enough time to sneak a hand down and take hold of Iesu's cock for a second time. It was crazy how right it felt to hear him whimper, to feel the silky heat of him shoving through the tunnel of his fingers. He tightened his grip and Iesu kissed him harder, all teeth and tongue as his dick added to the mess with a load worthy of an alpha.

And Sergi held on through it, even when his thrusts started to slow and he shivered against Sergi, clearly too sensitive to keep going but too turned on to stop himself from chasing pleasure a little way further.

Finally, he buried his face into Sergi's neck and pulled on his arm to signal he'd had enough. Sergi pulled his hand away and let it fall by his side on the bed—not like it mattered if he got a little more come on it.

Iesu was heavy on top of him—the guy was only slightly smaller than him and all muscle—and he was hot after all the exercise, but he wouldn't have pushed a girl off after sex, and it felt... He didn't have time to consider the etiquette because Iesu raised his head and pulled Sergi's left hand up to his mouth, then sucked his thumb into his mouth in one go, swallowing his own come with a pleased smile.

Sergi stared, thumb suddenly throbbing, but he couldn't think of anything to say before the other alpha rolled off and lay down next to him with a satisfied sigh.

"Told you," he said, voice a little rough, and Sergi had *just come,* but he still couldn't help but imagine what he'd sound like after sucking something considerably bigger for considerably longer.

"Fuck off," he replied, but he sounded so relaxed it only got Iesu to laugh.

Chapter 3

"I have an idea," Iesu said.

They were insulating the outer walls of the house—a task Gabriel had entrusted to them only after watching them do it properly three times each—so it was okay to stop to give him a look. It turned out sleeping with Iesu was only slightly less distracting than insurmountable sexual frustration.

Iesu raised his hands. "Hear me out first!"

Sergi shot him an unimpressed look. "Yeah, sure, like you would not just come right out and say it if it wasn't completely nuts."

Iesu huffed. "It's about Ray, so, I dunno, maybe it'll make you go all alpha on me or something."

Sergi hesitated, a little hurt. It was true his instincts towards Ray seemed somehow stronger than Iesu's. Or maybe it was just that Iesu wasn't freaked out by them, he took it all as given and worked with it like he'd done it all before. "Just say it," he snapped, going back to stretching the insulating layer against the brick.

"Well, Ray is... Well, he's not comfortable, right? So, if we go to see him together... It'd be faster."

Sergi froze in place, so shocked that for a moment he didn't know how to feel at all. "You think—"

"It's just an idea!" Iesu added hurriedly. He sounded so worried that Sergi turned to face him.

"Is it... is it really for Ray?" he asked carefully. He didn't want to offend Iesu, but it sounded a lot more like a sexual fantasy than a practical solution.

Iesu huffed and put down the hammer, breathing out slowly. "I—I don't know. I *want it*, okay? I'm not pretending it isn't the hottest thing I can imagine, because it is. But I think... I think it would help. He's stopped pretending we aren't there, but he looks exhausted all the time."

Sergi gave himself a minute by attaching another nail. "Maybe it's better, when I go second he's always... He seems really out of it."

"Yeah," Iesu agreed, voice low and sad. "I don't know how else... We can try, right? And if he doesn't want to, we won't, obviously."

"Okay," Sergi conceded. It was the best they could come up with, really.

The beer didn't do anything to help them relax and the werewolf-grade alcohol they brewed in their old pack wasn't easy to get—they couldn't spare the money nor the time to do anyone favours. So they made do with beer and whatever cans or bottles got damaged in the gas station where Josh worked.

It was nice anyway, after spending so long cramming themselves up in Gabriel's tiny living room just to spend time together, the new house—unfinished and rough as it was—felt like a luxury.

The furniture was from Salvation Army, but they'd sprung for new covers, and the previous owners must have been pretty careful because although the sofas smelt like humans, there was no food or animal scents at all. Sergi had possibly one of the keenest noses in the pack and he didn't think he'd be able to identify whoever had sat in his favourite new armchair if he met them in the street.

Josh was out, so of course, Gabriel and Iesu were doing most of the speaking. Alec was watching the movie, but he kept his laptop open in front of him anyway—maybe he felt like he should have been working even this late at night—so he had an excuse. Sergi couldn't quite keep up with whether Gabriel was teasing or actually telling them off most of the time, so he preferred to leave Iesu to it. He'd grown up with people who liked talking way more than he did, he was used to letting them fill the silence.

Ray whimpered quietly, turning around on the sofa in which he'd curled up half an hour earlier. He'd been even quieter than usual all day, but Sergi tried to give him space until he asked for something—there was so much Ray had lost control of already...

But now he couldn't keep back the question. "Ray, are you okay?"

Ray turned his face so it was no longer buried in the cushions and grimaced. "Cramps," he said shortly.

"Oh," Sergi stared for a moment. In truth, he had no idea how to help: werewolves didn't get sick, and even if he'd grown up attending human school and surrounded by their vulnerable non-shifting counterparts, the most he'd picked up was that you took aspirin for headaches and hot tea when you had a cold. "Maybe Alec...?"

The other alpha looked up at once. "What?"

"Cramps? Is there anything he can take for it?"

Alec looked almost flustered for a second before his professional manner took over. "Well, I don't know how any human medicine would work out for you and I don't have any here. But rubbing your belly might help. It's probably just gas."

Ray groaned and hid his face in the cushions again. Alec just stared at him, obviously not sure how to reconcile the facts with Ray's embarrassment.

"Is it hard to do?" Iesu asked. At some point he'd started listening to the conversation. Gabriel muted the TV.

"No," Alec replied. "You just press gently and rub in circles starting at the belly button. Clockwise."

Iesu stepped closer to Ray and put a gentle hand on his shoulder. "Hey, you wanna try that out?"

Ray remained curled up and Iesu glanced up and shot Gabriel a meaningful look, then gestured towards the TV. The sound went back on right in the middle of a fight scene. Alec flinched a little before settling and pointedly turning his attention back to the movie. Gabriel had already left the room, loudly announcing they needed more food. Iesu knelt down by the sofa, and Sergi turned his head just enough not to be obvious about watching.

Iesu was slowly rubbing Ray's back, leaning in close to whisper into his ear—so softly not even Sergi, who was closest, could catch anything but the cadence of his speech.

It took a few minutes, but by the time the movie had got interesting enough to capture Sergi's attention again, Ray had pushed himself up and allowed Iesu to cover him with a blanket. Sergi almost couldn't hide his shock in time when he saw Iesu wedging his way in between Ray and the back of the sofa, and Ray leaning back into him with a tired sigh.

He looked away but couldn't keep his gaze on the screen for long. Despite the blanket, the movement of Iesu's hand was quite distinctly a circular motion—he'd somehow talked Ray into it. Ray was leaning back against him, going visibly limp with relief. Iesu could have watched the TV from that angle, but his attention was focused on the man in his arms. At least until he looked up and caught Sergi's eyes. Sergi's heart skipped a beat, startled at being caught, but Iesu just smiled at him, happy and pleased.

It was completely crazy, but it took Sergi a whole thirty seconds to look down and check on Ray.

He was either sleeping or very close to it, and more importantly, the belly massage was working. He no longer looked grumpy and unhappy. It was like a small miracle, performed by a combination of Sergi noticing, Alec's medical advice and Iesu's daring to risk displeasing Ray for Ray's own good. And Ray's own strength, too—Sergi wasn't stupid enough to miss that, for all that alphas were meant to be strong, it fell on Ray to fight his own inclinations to become the centre of their new pack.

What was fighting an enemy compared to fighting yourself every step of the way?

It was just the beginning and things were hard enough, but watching Iesu push Ray's hair off his face and Ray turn his face into the touch... Sergi could almost believe they'd be okay.

I t was easy.

That was the crazy thing, really, not that he was fucking around with an alpha and it was great, but how easy it was to meet up and end up in bed together. Or behind a tree—Iesu either had a bit of an exhibitionist streak or didn't give any fucks about getting caught.

"I'm gay, mate," he told him when Sergi couldn't help but ask. "I got over all my hang-ups like, a decade ago."

"Doesn't mean you want people to catch you at it!"

Iesu raised an eyebrow at him. "We are in the middle of nowhere, and the only people who live here are werewolves with both superhearing and supernoses; only reason to catch us is if they want a free show."

He had a point, sure, but it still didn't sit quite right with Sergi for some reason. When he didn't answer, Iesu shrugged. "You can owe me one," he said.

"What?" Sergi jumped. "No way," he objected and tugged Iesu back behind the small grouping of trees where he'd gone to his knees for Sergi. "I was just saying, I'm not..."

Iesu watched him sceptically right until Sergi shoved him against a thick tree trunk and got to his knees. The ground was wet from the rain that morning—it'd be absolutely obvious they'd both been on their knees—and Iesu was hard under his tongue when he pressed his face right into his denim-covered crotch.

"G—Goddess!" Iesu dug his nails into the tree behind him, maybe wary of marking him up again. The scratches had hurt a bit, but it wasn't like they hadn't healed fast, and seeing Iesu lose control like that... but Sergi couldn't exactly ask for them, either.

He popped the button and lowered the zip, unable to resist pressing the flat of his tongue against the white underwear to get a hint of Iesu's taste. It made Iesu jump under his tongue.

He had never done this before, but... he'd thought about it. He had thought about it so much he was almost embarrassed it'd taken him this long to actually do it. What was the point of not doing what you wanted when you knew you wanted it? It didn't make him any less... attracted to men. Just an idiot trying to cover up the goddamned truth.

He didn't allow himself time to hesitate, just got Iesu's beautifully engorged cock out and sucked the head into his mouth. Salty and thick, just like his own. The other alpha jerked above him, like he was barely keeping himself in place, and for a moment, the idea of getting his face fucked stopped Sergi cold in his tracks—he was already half-hard again.

He pressed his thumbs against Iesu's hipbones, caressing the underside of his dick with his tongue and swallowing the salty, sticky pre-come. He couldn't say he enjoyed the taste, exactly, but... he glanced up, right past Iesu's heaving chest—shirt sticking to his perky nipples—and at his upturned chin where he'd left his whole throat exposed. Vulnerable and at his mercy.

And blowing a guy was supposed to be *submissive*.

He wondered what Iesu would do if he took him deeper, and then he tried it. Iesu swore, or at least he had to assume that was what the foreign words were. They sounded sweet despite the harshness of Iesu's voice—throat still a little raw from taking Sergi's cock—and Sergi closed his eyes and sucked him harder. He choked a little when Iesu lost control of his hips and thrust too hard, but it was just for a second. He shoved him back, swallowing the mix of saliva and come and leaning in for more, trying to use his tongue to keep things interesting without cutting off his air supply.

Not that Iesu seemed to need anything fancy; once he'd started speaking, he seemed unable to stop. Sergi thought he might have taken a turn towards the complimentary, and if it hadn't been so fucking hot to hear the half-broken sounds, he'd have complained about being unable to understand.

It wasn't until his jaw started aching that he remembered Iesu putting his hand at the base of Sergi's cock while he sucked. Sergi did the same. Iesu stopped speaking, and Sergi glanced up to see him biting his lip, frozen in place like he was one good stroke away from coming his brains out.

So he gave it to him, moved his hand through the slippery mix of his own spit and Iesu's precome and sucked at the same time. Whatever Iesu claimed, nobody needed superhearing to catch his scream as he came, but Sergi was too busy trying to swallow to care if half the county came down and took photos.

He didn't quite manage, it was too thick and there was too much of it. He had to pull back and spit on the ground, coughing a little. He looked back up, worried Iesu might take offense, but the other alpha was still panting, fingers buried up to the first knuckle into the wood of the unfortunate tree Sergi had chosen to support his weight. It looked like that was the only reason he was still upright.

He certainly didn't seem in any state to worry about whether his partner had followed blowjob protocol. Sergi found himself on his feet before he knew it, and Iesu's eyes blinked open, dazed and unfocused. They kissed like it was the only possible answer to being this close, and at some point Iesu managed to pull his nails back enough to get the use of his hands back and shoved one down Sergi's trousers once more. Sergi kissed him harder and let him; what was a little more mess at this point?

Afterwards, he rested his weight against Iesu, the only warm point in the cold of the night. He didn't move until Iesu rubbed his back and reminded him they had to get back for dinner.

Chapter 4

I t was easy until they moved into the new house together. There was no way anyone could miss they were sleeping together when they all spent every day in the same space. They hooked up a couple times in the shower, but even that would probably end up with them being found out—and Sergi felt guilty about using up too much hot water even if Iesu insisted they were using both of their rations.

So they stopped, which worked out great except that it made Sergi snappish as fuck. Josh, Gabriel and Alec had taken the fact that Ray couldn't have sex with them this late into the pregnancy as well as could be expected, but for Sergi, the cut-off seemed a lot more abrupt. And pointless too, because Iesu was going equally stir-crazy on the other side of his non-soundproofed bedroom wall, and he'd made it clear that he did not mind anyone knowing. So he wasn't just frustrated, but it was also his fault for being too scared to go for what he wanted.

And then Ray had shifted in his sleep and woken up in fur—a sure sign the pups would be arriving soon—and Sergi was happy, of course. But also fucking terrified. He wanted to talk to Iesu about it, but he didn't know how to *be* in a room with the guy and not jump his bones, not when he was already trying to crawl out of his own skin.

It was a blessing when Iesu decided he'd had enough, shoved right into his room without knocking, and demanded, "Come run with me."

Sergi gaped for all of three seconds before rolling off his bed, already half hard, and trying to walk out of the room. Iesu extended an arm in front of him. "Clothes," he said curtly. "Come meet me outside."

He slammed the door on his way out, and Sergi had to tug his wolf back from doing anything stupid at the disrespect.

By the time he managed to get his brain out of the gutter and his clothes more or less piled up on his chest of drawers, he had to open the window so he could jump out once he shifted. No way did he want to leave the house through the front door in the state he was in.

Iesu wasn't outside but he'd left a clear scent trail for him to follow. His wolf was torn between fucking his brains out and biting him into submission for barging in. He was fairly sure he could make sex more appealing than fighting, but in any case, he had to find him first.

Iesu was too clever to make it easy on him, so by the time he got to the forested area towards the back of their territory, Sergi was more curious than anything. He'd also caught a rabbit on his way and satiated some of the wolf's bloodthirstiness. He dropped the rest of the carcass at Iesu's feet, and his wolf preened when the food was accepted.

It was all wrong: Iesu wasn't a mate he should provide for. But maybe the wolf was confused by all the sex they'd been having, or maybe it was enough that Iesu was pack.

Sergi didn't have time to analyse it because as soon as he was done swallowing, Iesu shifted back. He had grass in his hair for some reason, and Sergi found himself on hands and knees without realising he'd pushed the wolf down and taken over.

Iesu gave him a sharp, pleased smile from where he was crouching. "Come here," he said.

And even though he was being a demanding little shit, Sergi shoved him down onto the grass and sealed their mouths together, his whole body relaxing into the warmth of him. He'd missed this, he had needed... Iesu shoved a knee between his legs and rubbed his cock against Sergi's belly. Sergi pushed right back and soon they had a rhythm: tongues tangling, hands roaming and the slickness growing between their bodies.

The first time was enough to take the edge off—enough to get them to trot to the river for a good, long drink. But it was nowhere near enough after so long, and soon they needed to find cover again.

"Wait, wait," Iesu asked between panting kisses. Sergi stopped. He was lying between Iesu's spread knees, which got them both some much needed stimulation. "Let's try this..." Iesu said in a careful tone and pushed Sergi until he knelt, then even further until he dismounted. Iesu closed his legs, pressing his thighs close together, then tugged him back onto his lap. "Lie down."

Sergi obeyed, more confused than anything else, and let Iesu rearrange his cock until he... *Fuck*. He'd put Sergi's cock between his own thighs, the silky skin there was a little too dry against the sensitive head, but... Sergi clenched his eyes shut as Iesu squeezed him hard.

He let out a sound, maybe an attempt at a word, he didn't know. It was all he could do to hold himself up enough not to crush the other alpha.

"Good?" Iesu asked, sounding smug enough that he had to know the answer. "Push," he ordered, and Sergi did as he was told, no questions asked. It felt... It wasn't fucking, too dry for that, but it felt...

"Dry," he managed to pant out.

"Oh, yeah," Iesu agreed, then shoved a hand back down, and when he wrapped it around his cock, Sergi realised he must have licked it. He almost came right then but Iesu squeezed him too hard. "Shhh... Not yet."

He took his hand away again, leaving Sergi cradled between the hot softness of his thighs.

"Ff— Fuck you," Sergi spat, trembling so hard his right arm gave up on him and his mouth ended up on Iesu's neck. He had to bite his lip not to put his mouth to it—the wolves gave them a lot of leeway, but there were some lines that weren't worth smudging.

Maybe Iesu could feel it, because he bent his elbows to bring up his torso and demanded, "Kiss me."

Sergi gave it to him, his mouth and his cock shoving desperately into the wet heat of his body. He wanted... He wanted everything, he wanted his mouth and his arse and his hands and his tongue and his *cock*. Iesu rolled them onto their sides, holding onto his side and his arse, and shoving his own cock against Sergi's abs even as Sergi's started spurting between his legs.

Sergi groaned, overwhelmed but unable to *stop*. He needed more, always more, of this, of... Iesu's breath hitched and he shuddered in his arms, and a moment later, he pushed Sergi onto his back and pressed his cock harder against him, messy and uncoordinated and out of control. Sergi held him steady as his own body came down from his peak, kissing his bruised lips softly until Iesu turned his face and whimpered, the wet, liquid heat of his seed spilling between their bodies.

Somehow, even though he shouldn't have been able to think, Iesu kept himself upright over him. Sergi couldn't stand the distance. He pulled him down, naked chests flush together, Iesu's come making their cocks slide against each other. They shuddered, but neither of them moved away. Iesu rested his face on Sergi's chest and Sergi held him in place.

Epilogue

"I'm freaking out," Iesu said.

He didn't sound it at all, and Sergi turned to look at him. It was a little weird to be having this conversation naked, but then again, they needed the privacy for this as much as for the fucking.

"About Ray?" he asked. Not because he had any idea.

Iesu frowned at him. "Yeah, what else is there?"

This, Sergi thought. He shrugged. "You just don't seem it."

Iesu shrugged. "Poker face."

"Okay," Sergi said. "Why are you freaking out?"

"I know he'll be okay, but..." He swallowed, and for the first time, Sergi could see beyond his confident façade. "But I'm going to be a *dad*. How am I... I don't know how to do that," he admitted.

"Ray knows," Sergi offered. "You saw his siblings, and Josh says Ray practically raised them."

Iesu huffed, rolling over on the grass and burying his face into his folded arms. "So we just leave it to him? How is that fair?"

"What? No!" He huffed and shoved the other alpha lightly. "We learn from him, idiot."

"Isn't that giving him more work too?" Iesu insisted almost petulantly.

"Only for a little bit," Sergi argued, feeling oddly like their roles had been reversed. "And I have changed diapers and stuff, so it'll just be you being totally useless."

"Oh, thanks," Iesu said, shooting him a look. He was trying for dry but missed it by a mile.

Sergi smiled back at him. "Oh, shut up. Just carpe diem it, okay? It's been working great so far."

It must have been the right thing to say because Iesu started laughing, and that was a sound Sergi never wanted to stop.

[End interlude 1.1]

The next book in the series is...

Alpha for the Pack: Ray wasn't ready to become an omega, but he's come to accept his fate... until it seems the pack might need even more of him than he can give.

Other Books by N.J. Lysk

The Stars of the Pack:

1) **Omega for the Pack** – When Ray presents as an omega instead of an alpha, his life changes forever. As a male omega, he's expected to mate with a select group of alphas and start a pack of his own. **A/B/O, M/M/M/M/M/M, M/M, mpreg, dubcon.** *Also in German, French, Italian & Portuguese.*

1.1) Simpler than Most *(an interlude)* – Sergi has stopped lying to himself: he's had a crush on a guy for a while. But it turns out telling yourself the truth is just the first step of a long journey. *Also in Spanish, German, Italian & French bilingual editions.*

2) **Alpha for the Pack** – Ray wasn't ready to become an omega, but he's come to accept his fate... until it seems the pack might need even more of him than he can give.

3) **Protectors of the Pack** – Alec and Gabriel are Ray's alphas first and foremost and nothing to each other. But three years ago... things were very different.

4) **Beloved of the Pack** – An omega is essential to his pack. But an omega is just a man. And a man needs to be loved. *Can you share your body and not share your heart?*

5) **Betas Aside** – Marisa never hesitated to go to her brother's aid—even when he has what she wants most in the world and can never have. But maybe where there's love, there is a way.

1) **Runt of the Litter** – An older omega who is ready to change the world, a young alpha who doesn't believe in his own potential; a love that's stronger than distance, age or inclination. **A/B/O. M/M. Age gap. Long-distance.**

2) **Paper Kisses** – Abel's not the kind of alpha to make a fuss when his omega ex gets together with someone else, but he's still lonely enough to seek out their kid's teacher to complain about wasting time to celebrate Valentine's day. He doesn't expect to find a lot more than paper hearts. **M/M. Age gap. Human/werewolf. Sweet.**

Rules to Break:

- **Not Destiny** – Thomas and Uriel were never meant to be together. If they choose each other anyway, can they beat the odds? **An Alpha/Beta romance.**
- **Cracking Ice series (7 episodes)** – Hockey means everything to them both... Until they meet each other. **An Alpha/Omega hockey romance.**
- **A Unique Perspective** (*Coming soon*) – Yadriel doesn't look like an omega, but to the eyes of a very interested beta photographer, maybe there is a lot more to him than his size. **A beta/omega BDSM romance.**

Standalones:

- **A Light in Winter** – Alone and trapped by a dangerous arctic storm, two young men have no choice but to confront their feelings for each other. **A/B/O. Cousins. Werewolves. Isolation.**
- **The Omega Sacrifice** - *Fate deals the cards, but you can still play your hand.* When a young omega is sent away to marry a strange alpha, he has no choice but to face who he is. **An arranged marriage omegaverse romance.**
- **A Bond Unbroken** – When Lia presents as an omega, her best friend offers her anything she needs. But Lia's been in love with Amira for years and whatever her wolf wants, her heart cannot take what's not freely given. **Best friends to lovers. F/F. A/B/O.** *Also in*

Spanish, German, Italian & French.

- **Truth Unveiled:** When Kala comes out at work to spite her biphobic coworker, she ends up in need of a fake date for the Christmas party. Her best friend immediately offers to help, but for how long can they handle the pretence? **F/F. Shifters, not A/B/O. A best friends fake dating novella.**

- **Omega Under The Moon** – School is over and Cole is ready to take a break before adult life starts, but when a camping trip with his two best mates turns into something much wilder, it'll change his life forever. **A/B/O. M/M/M.** *Also in French, German & Italian.*

- **Omega On A Mission** - omegas are carers, not fighters, and Gabi is happy looking after his alpha. But when he comes across an animal in danger, his protective instincts flare up, and nobody wants to get in the way of an omega on a mission. **A/B/O.**

Intertwined Fates:

- **Not to be Borne** – When his twin brother presents as an omega, Michuá feels like the world is ending. In a way, becoming an omega himself seems like the only way to stay together... But Zybyn's new alpha wants a lot more than they have bargained for and in a journey towards a strange land, there is nothing to stop him from taking it. **Non-con, abuse, twincest, HEA.**

- **His, Truly** – When Shane unexpectedly presents as an omega during the full moon, his twin brother steps

in to protect him from the alphas who'd claim him...
But Tim is also an alpha. **A/B/O. M/M. Twincest.**
Also in French & German.

- **The Realm of the Impossible** – The Queen is dead
and Lorax is ready to take his rightful place when an
intimate betrayal leaves him with no choice but to
surrender his throne or lose his only remaining family.
At this unbearable crossroad, Lorax can watch the
new Queen lead his country to a war that will destroy
it, or indulge his enemy's sole weakness: himself. **A
Taboo M/M Royal Romance.**

Werewolves of Windermere:

1) **The Mating Habits of Werewolves** – Devlin is
an omega with ambitions that have nothing to do
with alphas, but when destiny comes calling, he may
not have that much of a choice. **A/B/O, M/M/M,
mpreg.**

2) **Alphas Alone** – An alpha werewolf has some
responsibilities he can't ignore: finding an omega,
protecting his pack, not falling for another alpha.

3) **The Parenting Habits of Werewolves** – With
children in common, Devlin, Naveen and Rami
know their fates are bound together, but can they
find a balance beyond domesticity? And can they
build a love that can last? **The conclusion to the M/
M/M Mpreg Romance.**

Deep in the Dark – (Erotica by N.Y. Lysk):

- **The Weight of Duty** – Now that the twins are of age, their uncle takes them in hand to teach them their marital duties. But the experience will be very different for each of them. **Dub-con, feminization, medical body modification, abuse, group sex, arranged marriage, betrayal, incest.**

- **Soldier On** – When a humble young man is captured by the enemy lord during battle, he is expected to offer defeat to his captor by allowing him to bed him. But he is young enough that the act might unintentionally activate a hormonal process that will irreversibly feminise him. **Dub-con, Non-con, mpreg, feminization, debasement.**

- **The Will of Heaven** – Prince Hiram of Pradeira is deemed unfit to be king after his father dies. But as a direct descendant of the gods, only those of his bloodline can reign and so to avoid civil war, he agrees to have a child with each of the princes of the other noble houses of the kingdom so that his first born and heir can inherit the throne from whoever fathered him. **Dub-con, mpreg, feminization, medical kink, debasement.** *Also in German & Italian.*

- **His Brother's Dowry** – Tony agrees to accompany his brother to a new pack, knowing he will have to submit to alphas in the absence of omegas but willing to sacrifice his comfort to give Peter a chance to find love. But his brother is already in love with an omega girl and he will give anything to get her. Even Tony. **Dub-con, non-con, mpreg, feminization, debasement, body modification.**

- **The Alpha Solution** – Junen will be the next alpha of his pack... until one day he's taken by a stranger—an alpha his father rejected and who's determined to use Junen to get to him. By making him his omega. **Non-con, mpreg, kidnapping, feminization, fisting, debasement, body modification, group sex, abuse.**

About the author

N.J. Lysk (pronouns: whatever) is a queer one—in almost every sense of the word—for whom stories have always been their one true home. She studied linguistics and literature (which is to say, someone offered him a genuine excuse to read professionally) and ended up teaching, but writing is their one true love.

Addicted to angst, enamoured of mpreg and always ready to try a new kink (in a book, that's it!) she became hooked into the omegaverse through fanfic (but he doesn't have the patience to write other people's characters) and has recently expanded from werewolves to hockey players.

If your heart veers towards the dark, look for N.Y. Lysk instead & subscribe to the Dark & Taboo list[1] (these books all come with serious warnings!).

Join their mailing list at **www.njlysk.com/newsletter**[2] for book updates and free books, updates and more cool things.

Books can be acquired directly from the website at a reduced rate—new releases also become available there earlier.

---

1. https://readerlinks.com/l/3218963

2. **http://www.njlysk.com/newsletter**